Snowboarding
to the EXTREME!

Snowboarding to the EXTREME!

Bill Gutman

TOR®

A Tom Doherty Associates Book / New York

SNOWBOARDING: TO THE EXTREME!

Cover photographs © 1997 by Shawn Frederick
Interior photographs © 1997 by Shawn Frederick

This book is printed on acid-free paper.

A Tor® Book
Published by Tom Doherty Associates, Inc.
175 Fifth Avenue
New York, NY 10010

Tor® is a registered trademark of Tom Doherty Associates, Inc.

Library of Congress Cataloging-in-Publication Data

Gutman, Bill.
    Snowboarding : to the extreme! / Bill Gutman.
        p.   cm.
    "A Tom Doherty Associates book."
    ISBN 0-312-86255-5
    1. Snowboarding.   I. Title.
GV857.S57G88   1997
796.9—dc21   97-13795
                                        CIP

First Edition: October 1997

Printed in the United States of America

0 9 8 7 6 5 4 3 2 1

ACKNOWLEDGMENTS

The author would like to thank the following people for taking time from busy schedules to share their knowledge of snowboarding and their feelings about this new and exciting sport. Rick Waring, Bob Gille, Shannon Dunn, Don Szabo, and Shannon Melhuse are all involved in different aspects of snowboarding and are champions in their own right.

Also a special thanks to Shawn Frederick, who not only supplied all the fine photos that accompany the text, but also took a great deal of time to explain many of the disciplines and techniques of a sport in which he participates as well as photographs.

For their help and contributions to *Snowboarding: To the Extreme!,* the photographer gives special thanks to Jay Wailer of MISTRAL Snowboards, Kris Bowers of OAKLEY Sunglasses, and Nevin Sport Systems.

CONTENTS

Snowboarding TO the EXTREME!

MONTY ROACH SHOWING STYLE WITH HIS FRONTSIDE NOSE-BONE
AT A-BASIN, COLORADO.

INTRODUCTION

I T'S a sport that can be relaxing and soothing—a solitary boarder carving slowly down a snow-covered mountain on a sunny winter's day. It can also be athletic, with twists and spins and handstands in the halfpipe. Or it can be exciting—two competitors racing side by side down a giant slalom course. Then there is the rugged fun of boarder-cross, the challenge of freeriding down an obstacle course, or the streetstyle boldness of sliding along logs and leaping over rocks. And finally there is the thrilling but risky rush of an extremist, plunging into unknown territory on the top of an untamed and often unconquered mountain.

All of the above describe a single sport—snowboarding. And it just may be the fastest-growing sport in the United States today.

While snowboarding is a close relative to skiing, it has a totally different philosophy and a different feel. In fact, in many ways the sport evolved more from surfing and skateboarding than from skiing, but its allure is becoming universal. Many skiers who have crossed over to snowboarding have never put their skis on again. And many snowboarders, experiencing the special rush and excitement that comes from the sport, have in turn tried their hand at surfing and found that riding a huge wave is similar to riding down a snow-covered mountain.

Top professional snowboarder Don Szabo began his career as a skateboarder and then skied for five years before taking up snowboarding. It's not hard to see which sport has become his favorite.

"Going down a mountain skiing, you're straight forward," Szabo says. "You have two separate sticks under your feet. You don't feel as whole, as one, as you do with your snowboard. Snowboarding is a more flowing, all together feeling. You're all at one with your board."

Snowboarding is just like its name says. You ride on a single board, your feet buckled into bindings in a way similar to skis. But unlike skiing,

1 JIMMY HALOPOFF SNOWBOARDING ON A DAY WITH EXCEPTIONALLY GOOD SNOW.

you have no poles to help you with your balance. With two skis and a pair of ski poles to manage, a person can suddenly find his body going in every direction at once. The snowboarder *is* truly one with his board. Yet he can achieve all the discipline of a skier and more.

Snowboarding offers something for everyone, from a recreational weekend athlete, to a competitive racer, to an extremist daredevil. It is a sport that has grown so rapidly since the late 1980s that Alpine slalom racing on snowboards may soon be part of the Winter Olympic Games.

But Alpine slalom racing isn't the only way to go on a snowboard. Recreational boarders may simply enjoy a long, slow *carve* down a mountain, going from side to side in large, looping S-shaped turns. Those who come from a skateboarding background usually prefer the halfpipe. They ride their boards up and down a pair of facing ramps made of snow, doing stunts and tricks as they reach the top of each side.

Some prefer an obstacle course, going off the manicured mountain slopes and riding among fallen trees and rocks, jumping and sliding across whatever might be in their way. And many snowboarders are beginning to enjoy the fun and the challenge of boarder-cross, which is a race among four to eight riders down an obstacle course, almost like a combination of motocross and Roller Derby. You can bump, push, and shove the competition; the object is to be the first across the finish line.

Extreme snowboarders have taken the sport one step beyond. They long to challenge the unknown, often traveling by backpack or even helicopter to a lonely, steep mountaintop where they often find the ride and the risk of their lives. This style isn't for amateurs, but a growing number of experienced snowboarders are beginning to look a lot more closely at this ultimate challenge.

If snowboarding sounds like a fascinating sport, it is. That's why the converts keep coming—from skiing, surfing, skateboarding, and other sports. And with the increasing popularity of the sport that now finds skiers sharing the slopes with snowboarders, many are starting from scratch, with no crossover sport to give them a jump-start. Ski resorts now rent snowboards with the same frequency they rent skis.

This book is both for beginners—who want to learn the basics of the sport and how to get started—and for those who just want to become better acquainted with the various disciplines of the sport. The teachers here are some of the top professionals in snowboarding today. Snowboarding is like a good book: Once you get into it, it's hard to put down. Professional snowboarder Shannon Dunn is a prime example. She was a skier for thirteen years, beginning the sport at the age of three. Then when she was about sixteen, her brother introduced her to the world of snowboarding. She strapped herself onto the board, rode it down the mountain, and her life was never quite the same.

"Snowboarding was just totally different," Shannon Dunn says. "I loved it so much that I haven't skied once since I got on a snowboard for the first time."

PART ONE

1991 UNITED STATES HALFPIPE CHAMPION JIMI SCOTT AT
SNOW SUMMIT, CALIFORNIA.

A SNOWBOARDING HISTORY

I N a way, it's kind of amazing that snowboarding didn't become a popular sport much sooner. A number of similar crossover sports have been in existence for centuries, in one form or another. For example, scratched on the walls of ancient caves are pictures of people wearing crude skis. These homemade skis were used mainly for transportation in snowy climates.

Back in the nineteenth century, mailmen used skis to reach snowy mountain camps in the western United States, while gold miners and ranchers also used skis for transportation, and eventually, for sport. Then, in the late-nineteenth century, an Austrian named Mathias Zdarsky invented the first ski poles and shortened the length of the skis. Before long, Alpine competition began. Yet it would take nearly another full century for someone to realize a similar effect could be achieved by riding a single board instead of two skis.

It was the same with surfing. No one made the connection between surf and snow for centuries. People living in the South Pacific have been surfing for hundreds of years. When Captain James Cook, the English navigator and explorer, reached Hawaii in 1778, he discovered surfing—a competitive sport with prizes offered to the winners of contests. The sport really began to get popular in parts of the United States in the 1950s, and the United States Surfing Association was formed in 1961. But it would still be another quarter-century before people seriously began to transfer this simple concept of man and board to the snow.

Of course there were always crude attempts at what is today called snowboarding. Nearly every kid who owned a sled at one time or another has tried going down a hill standing up on it. That made the sled a snowboard with runners. But it wasn't until the mid-1960s that someone finally made a board for the express purpose of sliding down a snow-covered hill with a passenger standing on it.

Sherman Poppen designed the board known as the "Snurfer." It's not difficult to figure out the meaning of the name—a combination of snow and surf. The Snurfer was simply a piece of plywood shaped roughly like a surfboard and it came with a rope leash. The leash could be used to pull the board up the hill; then it helped the rider hold on during the trip down.

However, there was one obvious problem. It was nearly impossible for the rider to control the board. It didn't turn well and there was no way to control either speed or direction. So if you ventured onto a steep hill with a Snurfer in tow, you had to prepare for a wild, uncontrolled ride to the bottom and hope you could make it down in one piece and without wiping out.

To many, the Snurfer was little more than a toy, something for a youngster to use on a not-too-steep hill near his home. Yet more than a million of these rudimentary boards were sold in the space of a few years. The brief popularity of Snurfers, however, really didn't foreshadow the development of a major sport.

At the same time that Sherman Poppen was developing the Snurfer in the mid-1960s, another new fad was sweeping much of the country. The first wave of skateboarders had begun traversing the streets and sidewalks of many towns and cities. But in some sections of the country, the snow and ice of winter made skateboarding almost impossible at times. That made a New Jersey teenager named Tom Sims very angry. He wanted to skate all year round.

Sims began playing with the design of his skateboard in wood-shop class at his school. He decided to modify the board so it could be used on ice. It wasn't until 1969 that Sims came up with a board that resembled the snowboards of today. It no longer had wheels, but was flat on the bottom. He also added bindings so that the rider's feet could be strapped to the board.

Another early innovator of the sport was Carl Ekstrom of La Jolla, California. While Tom Sims was working on his design in New Jersey, Ekstrom also was making early versions of snowboards on the West Coast. He is generally credited with shaping the first asymmetrical boards. These were thinner in the middle than at the ends, a design that helped with turning and maneuverability. So, slowly but surely, and on both the East and West Coasts, the modern snowboard was born.

But the sport didn't take off immediately. On the contrary, at first it met more resistance than acceptance. The memory of out-of-control Snurfers was still on people's minds. Snurfers were such unreliable boards that many ski-resort operators faced liability insurance problems and actually had to ban the boards from their slopes. Even though the new boards in no way resembled the Snurfer, acceptance came slowly.

Throughout the 1970s, the sport endured a difficult period. But all the while, manufacturers were looking to improve the design of the board, to make it safer and more maneuverable. By the early 1980s, things were improving. The first organized contests began to spring up. Dedicated snowboarders traveled from contest to contest, or from mountain to mountain, to compete and to demonstrate their sport. Slowly but surely, ski resorts began making a place for snowboarders, acknowledging that the sport was as safe or maybe safer than skiing, and that the two could co-exist side by side on the mountain.

More skiers, surfers, and skateboarders have begun trying the new sport, many of them finding it more attractive than their previous sport. Snowboarding is finally here to stay and, in the late 1990s, is on the brink of a real popularity explosion. The only surprising thing is that it didn't happen sooner.

ORGANIZED SNOWBOARDING

In many ways, snowboarding's history has been like a youngster experiencing rapid, almost uncontrolled growth in a short time. The sport has gone through a period of adjustment; the people involved are trying to put all the parts together so they work as a whole. That isn't always easy with a relatively new sport.

One of the prime movers in trying to bring snowboarding into the mainstream of big-time sports is Rick Waring, executive director of the Professional Snowboarding Tour of America (PSTA). Waring has a surfing background and still remembers some of the difficulties trying to organize that much-older sport.

"We tried to pull surfing into the 1984 Olympics which were held in Los Angeles," Waring says. "We wanted to run it as a demonstration competition at Malibu. What happened is that we got ripped off by a guy who said he had an organization with a huge membership and it turned out to be a Betty Crocker mailing list with just a few names on it. The Olympic Committee didn't want to risk embarrassment and didn't put it in."

Because of this experience, Rick Waring knew the danger signals and knew what had to be done to bring snowboarding into the mainstream of organized sports. He became involved with the sport in 1989, when a surfer friend of his urged him to try it. Besides enjoying the new sport, Waring saw the potential in it, but knew it had to be well organized.

He first became involved at the amateur level, becoming the director of the United States Amateur Snowboarding Association. Soon he was picking up experience by organizing amateur events in California. They ran both slalom and giant-slalom races and began holding some halfpipe contests as well. But even as late as 1989, Waring says the halfpipe performers didn't have a whole lot of skills. Everything was still relatively new.

There had already been a few organized events going on for years. Rick Waring calls them the "grandfather" events. One was the U.S. Open, hosted by a snowboard manufacturer and held at Stratton, Vermont, each year. But aside from the Open and some other select competitions, the organization of the sport was still weak.

The Open dated back to the early 1980s, and although there were a few professional snowboarders by that time, there wasn't much money available for prizes. Jeff Grell, who would later work with Rick Waring to organize the sport, ran an event in Aspen, Colorado, in the early days. It was called the Aspen Grand Prix, but the winners of the various events got only about one hundred dollars.

Around 1989, a number of new tours began to spring up all at once. Pretty soon they were competing with each other for top riders, and in a new sport, that isn't always good.

"There were financial problems caused by people trying to pull too many pieces together," Waring recalls. "It also caused scheduling conflicts. What I began seeing was a lot of snowboard manufacturers trying to pull together a tour so they could basically showcase their riders. So the money wasn't very big and there was no real effort to put the sport on television."

Rick Waring finally decided to do something about it. He felt that for snowboarding to have a strong identity, as well as a better national organization, certain things had to be done.

"I felt that half the battle was presentation," he says. "Remember, in snowboarding you're often up against the elements. There can be the wind and snow factor. So you had to be prepared for the worst.

"In addition, the competitors had to present a professional manner. They had to show up when scheduled, respect the mountain, the judges, the staff, and the other competitors. At that time, ski racers came in with their thousand-dollar snowsuits. But the snowboarders were considered the bad boys."

Because of his experience with surfing, Waring felt he knew which things had to be corrected with snowboarding.

"Once we came into the arena, we literally shoved a professional attitude down these snowboarders' throats. We went out to create champions with or without the so-called top riders. We didn't want a prima-donna attitude. We managed to begin getting the sport on television and that helped create new stars. Jimi Scott was the overall halfpipe champion and the world got to see the great skills of Craig Kelly."

Rick Waring's first tour was in 1989. Body Glove, a company that manufactures sportswear and wet suits, came in as a sponsor and Waring switched to organizing professional events. There were nine events with some $250,000 in prize money, as well as TV exposure via the Prime Network. In May, at the end of the season, a special event was held in Colorado. There was a total of $25,000 in prize money with individual winners getting checks for some $4,000. It doesn't sound like much compared with the big-time sports of today (baseball, basketball, tennis, etc.), but for snowboarding it was a leap forward.

By 1990, Rick Waring's tour was the only game in town and there was an increase in money, as well as commitments from all the major riders. The following year the recession knocked some sponsors out of the box and the prize money actually went down, but more corporate sponsors are once again showing interest and Rick Waring is confident that the sport will become even more organized in the upcoming years.

Besides Waring's Professional Snowboarding Tour, there is a world tour under the auspices of the International Snowboarding Federation, with stops in Japan, Europe, and the United States. Additionally the World Cup has become a major international event. In 1991, the stops were France, Japan, and Aspen, Colorado. Overall total points earned determined the world champions in both Alpine racing and freestyle.

Rick Waring feels the sport can only continue to grow. He would like to see a big push made to at least get the racing events into the 1998 Winter Olympics as a demonstration sport.

"I think we've got a good chance," Waring says. "The ski industry is beginning to support snowboarding because they see it as a viable income

2 1992 UNITED STATES ALPINE RACING CHAMPION SHANNON MELHUSE.

now. That helps. So I think you'll see the slalom and giant slalom come in first. A clear winner-loser situation is more understandable to people not familiar with the sport and is more suited to TV. I think the halfpipe will take a little longer, as did [the introduction of] freestyle skiing in the Olympics."

Halfpipe competition, however, has already had some television exposure and may not be that far away from a major breakthrough. Though it is a judged event, other sports such as figure skating and diving have been very successful as judged events.

Though snowboarding is a multifaceted sport, the organized tours are sticking mainly to slalom racing and halfpipe freestyle for now. Rick Waring acknowledges that freestyle obstacle-course riding is also an event that takes great skill, but he doesn't feel the public is ready for it.

"It puts the competitor at risk and really throws too many elements at the public for television exposure," Waring says. "In a sense, many people will look at obstacle-course riders and see a rebel, a kid sliding down their curb and hitting their mailbox. They see a skateboarder and equate it with that."

So the reputation of one sport can sometimes cross over into another as its competitors do. Streetstyle skateboarders have been battling a rebel image for years. Obstacle-course snowboarders commit the same kind of derring-do on their boards, only their course is confined to a snow-covered mountain. But again, as with any new sport, some elements take longer to gain acceptance than others.

Rick Waring sees the problem in the early 1990s as one of numbers. "We'll attract more than one hundred men to some of our events, but barely reach thirty women," he says. "I've stressed to the women as well as the men that corporate America is taking a strong look at our tour. Now that we've succeeded in coming back for a second year, everybody seems to want to get involved. So we've got to keep presenting an exciting and skilled package. That will get the good competitors on TV every week and we'll all begin making a lot more money."

The way the sports world and the business world must balance each other may seem strange to purists, but that's the way it works today. It was considered a major breakthrough, for instance, when Damian Sanders became the first snowboarder to make a McDonald's commercial. It also helped introduced snowboarding to many more people. And that's just what Rick Waring and the other people trying to organize the sport are looking for.

They seem to be winning their battle.

PART TWO

CRYSTAL ALDANA STYLES THROUGH A BASIC OLLIE AIR.

GETTING READY TO SNOWBOARD

THE BOARD

SNOWBOARDS have come a long way since the days of the Snurfer. The modern snowboard is a quality piece of equipment that will serve the boarder well. Because of its superior craftsmanship, it is not inexpensive. But people should not look to get off cheap anyway. It is a rule of thumb in any sport that even beginners should buy the best equipment they can possibly afford.

Although there are two different types of snowboards—the racing board and the freestyle board—both boards are constructed in the same basic way. The bottom is made from a material called Petex, the same substance used on quality skis. The edges are made from sharp stainless steel, which helps to reinforce the board as well as to dig into the snow.

The core of the board is generally made with vertical strips, or *stringers,* of lightweight balsa wood. Between the strips of wood is an ultralight foam. The combination of the balsa wood and foam makes the core of the board as light as can be. The top, or deck, of the board can be made from

3   FREESTYLE BOARD.

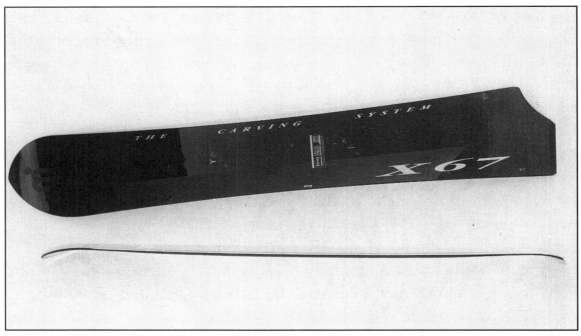

4   RACING BOARD.

several different types of materials. Perhaps the most popular is polyurethane, which is tough and durable. The board also has stainless steel inserts that hold the bindings in place.

There is a difference in shape and texture between the racing board and the freestyle board. All boards have a slight *camber* or rise in the middle. The camber gives them flexibility and movement when the rider weights and unweights during various maneuvers. But the racing boards are generally a bit stiffer and longer than the freestyle boards. They are also basically flat on the ends with more of a sidecut for sharp turns.

The sidecut actually refers to the shape of the side of the board. A board may, for instance, measure twelve inches wide at the nose and tail ends, but taper in so it's only nine or ten inches wide across the middle or the *waist,* as it's called. That taper is the sidecut. A longer sidecut allows for sharper turns. A giant-slalom racer constantly has to make sharp turns and needs the longer sidecut.

By contrast, the freestyle board is generally shorter and does not have as much of a sidecut. Riders operating in the halfpipe, for instance, do not have the need to make sharp turns. But their freestyle boards have a rise, or *kick,* at each end. In other words, the last few inches of board turn upward. This is very similar to the construction of freestyle skateboards.

Unlike skateboards and surfboards, which the rider simply stands on, snowboards use bindings to hold the rider's boots to the board. This is another reason to always buy a quality board. Some inexpensive and very lightweight boards have a core made completely from foam, without the wood strips. The danger with these boards is that the bolts used to hold the bindings in place can suddenly give way and pull out. If this happens during a fast run or in a sharp turn, the rider can easily suffer a knee or ankle injury, or the board can pop up and catch him anywhere, from the shin to the face.

Most boards are geared for the mature rider. Very young children beginning the sport might want to start with a small board. Rental shops usually carry one or two of these very small boards to every twenty regular boards.

After growing out of the real small boards, youngsters can find boards from 130 centimeters (51 inches) to 144 centimeters (56 inches). These are narrower than adult boards and the choice should be based on the youngster's size and weight. There is also a board in the 150 centimeter (60 inches) range. Freestyle boards are generally in the 155–165 centimeter range (62–66 inches). Racing boards are a bit longer, usually about 180 centimeters (70 inches) in length. But no matter what the size, make sure you get a quality board.

Prices have gone up as the boards have become more sophisticated. There was a time when $150 would buy a moderately good board. Now a board in the $400 price range is considered low-end. Part of the reason has been the general increase in the prices of all sporting equipment. The other is the higher-quality construction of today's boards.

So the low-end or even middle-range snowboard might suffice for a beginner. But the harder it is ridden, the quicker it will deteriorate. A less-than-the-best board will often crack after just half a season of rough riding. There are a number of other things that can happen, including the steel edges blowing out, something that can easily cause a fall and injury.

A quality board may cost $650 or more, but it is a board that will take a beginner a long way and even last several years for the expert. It's a decision every snowboarder must make. Sometimes you might find you don't have the money for a quality board. Then you have to make do and maybe buy yet another board the following year. But if you have the dollars, don't hesitate to buy the best snowboard you can. It will pay off in more ways than one.

BINDINGS, BOOTS, AND CLOTHING

While the board itself is obviously the most important piece of equipment needed for snowboarding, there are several other items a rider must have, and a few others that are optional. Once again, cost may be a factor, so be prepared. There is no cheap way to get started.

A pair of bindings is an absolute necessity. It is the bindings that hold the rider on the board, much as they hold a skier on his skis. There are two basic types of bindings. Most freestylers tend to use the *high-back bindings,* while racers will usually put a *plate binding* on their boards.

High-back bindings are made from a strong, rigid plastic and are spe-

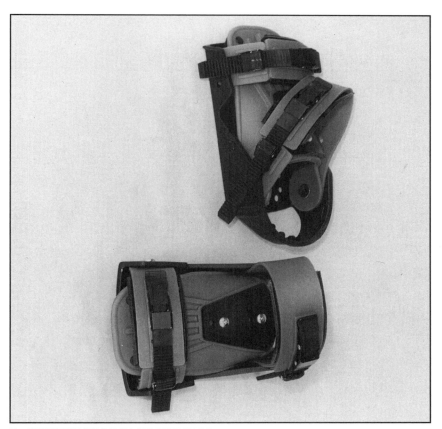

5 FREESTYLE (HIGH-BACK) BINDINGS.

cifically designed for use with soft boots. These are boots with leather on the top and rubber soles. The bindings fit over the boot and are held in place by two or three buckle clips. The rear support, a solid piece of plastic molded into the shape of the boot, comes up almost to the top of the boot.

Some freestylers have been known to create additional support by wrapping duct tape around the tops of their boots and the binding. This is something for experienced riders only. They want the additional support for some of their tricks and stunts, but they don't wrap the tape so tight that it restricts their movement.

The plate binding is made either from metal or from hard plastic, and has a toe and heel fastener called a *bail.* These bindings are designed to

6   HARD BOOTS WITH PLATE BINDINGS (USED MAINLY BY RACERS).

be used with a ski-type boot, which has a hard shell and an extended toe and heel. Plate bindings are generally more expensive than high-backs. Either will likely run more than $100, adding to the cost of the initial investment.

Boots are another item that the new snowboarder must consider. If you are using a racing board with plate bindings, there is only one choice; you must use the hard-shell ski-type boot with its extended toe and heel to hook into the bail. It's been said that this boot represents the only similarity between skiing and snowboarding. A good hard-shell boot will cost $200 or more.

With high-back bindings, riders will wear the soft boot with its leather upper and rubber soles. These boots are also expensive; a good pair is in

7 SOFT BOOT FOR FREESTYLERS.

the same price range as their hard-shell cousins. But there are a couple of advantages to soft boots: First, they can be worn for things other than snowboarding, such as hiking or simply walking.

Secondly, they often have a plastic shell on the inside of the boot. The majority of these shells are removable. Skiers, for instance, can take comfortable old shells from ski boots and put them into snowboarding boots. There is a trick to save some money: Buy the soft boot a size larger than your foot. Then buy a shell the size of your foot. That way, you can keep changing shells as they wear out without spending another $200 on new boots every couple of years.

Most snowboarders wear gloves because it's usually cold on the mountain.

8 SNOWBOARDING GLOVES.

Snowboarding gloves sometimes have longer cuffs than ski gloves and fit snugly over the jacket sleeve to keep the snow out. The recreational rider carving down the mountain can wear this type of glove.

Racers generally wear a glove that has extra padding across the back. This padding will protect the hands if they slap up against a gate on a sharp turn. It is recommended that freestylers wear gloves with the palms and fingertips made of Kevlar, the same material used in bulletproof vests. Since freestylers are often grabbing the edges of their boards, a plain glove is easily cut on the sharp metal edge. If the glove is sliced, chances are the rider's hand will be sliced as well. In fact a sharp edge can have the same effect as a knife. With Kevlar-reinforced gloves, this cannot happen.

The weather should be the determining factor for the remainder of the snowboarder's clothing. Temperatures on the mountain can vary greatly. Riders are out in both balmy and blizzard conditions. When it's cold it can be rough.

"When it's freezing cold, it's harder to do things and you don't really want to be out there at all," admits Shannon Dunn, the world-class competitive freestyler. "The extreme coldness makes you feel stiff. Competitors do better when it's warmer."

The beginner must consider this as well. There now are manufacturers making specific snowboarding clothes. Pants, for instance, can be purchased with both knee and buttocks padding built right in. But the experienced rider usually has his own favorite way of dressing.

As a rule of thumb, outer garments should always be waterproof. If your clothes become wet from falling on a cold day, they won't keep you warm. In subfreezing temperatures, several layers of clothing may be worn, beginning with thermal underwear. But don't wear so much that you'll lose your flexibility and ability to maneuver your board. Make sure you can still move freely.

9 FREESTYLE SNOWBOARDING SUIT.

So, clothes should be loose and lightweight, waterproof and insulated. In colder weather, a hat of some kind is an absolute must. Blue jeans and shorts are sometimes the choice of experienced boarders in milder weather, but this is not a good idea for beginners who will probably fall more often. These items absorb moisture and, once wet, will make it feel a lot colder than it is.

Two other pieces of advice. Snow and sun can present a glaring, sometimes blinding combination. Therefore, a good pair of goggles or sunglasses is advisable. Not only will it enable the rider to see better, but it will also screen out potentially harmful ultraviolet rays, which are more intense at higher elevations. So make sure your glasses provide ultraviolet (UV) protection.

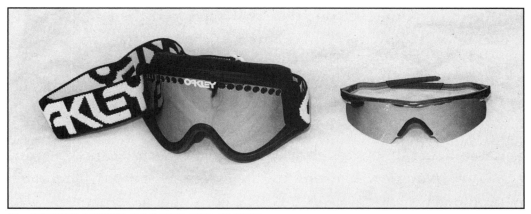

10 SNOWBOARDING GOGGLES AND GLASSES.

While no one expects the same kind of sunburn on a mountain as you would get on a beach, the combination of sun, snow, and wind can cause a nasty and possibly harmful burn. Once again, an ounce of prevention is worth a pound of cure. It's a good idea, therefore, to use a commercial sunscreen on *all* exposed areas of your skin. It's a small but worthwhile investment.

One quick word about another piece of equipment that generally has little place in traditional skiing or snowboarding: the helmet. With the normal disciplines such as Alpine racing and halfpipe, helmets are rarely worn. But in some of the newer disciplines, including certain obstacle courses, boarder-cross, and certainly in extreme snowboarding, a helmet is recommended.

All equipment and clothing should be regularly inspected for any kind of defect. It should be kept clean and dry when not in use. Boards, boots, and bindings should be wiped dry after each use. Otherwise, maintenance is minimal.

Snowboarding is not an inexpensive sport. People must sometimes travel substantial distances to reach the mountain. Beginners may rent equipment if they're not sure how they will take to the new sport. Once they decide to purchase their own, they must be prepared to spend a good sum of money for top equipment. But they will soon find their investment is a good one. It will allow them to fully enjoy a great sport.

SAFETY AND PITFALLS

Perhaps the first rule of thumb when talking about safe snowboarding is *don't do too much too soon.* Learning the sport is relatively easy and safe. But many people get a few basics under their belts and suddenly they want to do it all, go out and rip down a mountain or over an obstacle course. That's where the trouble can start.

"Snowboarding is so easy it's pathetic," says Shawn Frederick, an experienced snowboarder and one of the top photographers in the field. "But it becomes a lot more difficult when you get better simply because there are endless numbers of things you can do."

And therein lies an immediate danger. If an inexperienced snowboarder takes to an out-of-bounds obstacle course, he may suddenly find himself in trouble. What if he comes upon a sharp drop-off and picks up speed? He may not have the turning skills to avoid that onrushing tree at high speed. Or he may try to duplicate a freestyler he saw jump over a rock, slide down a log, or try to grab the board in midair. These are all basic freestyling maneuvers, but not for the beginner.

So while you may find snowboarding easy to learn, don't be fooled. Bring your level of skill up one step at a time. Try new things gradually and, as Shawn Frederick says, "Just ride and practice, practice, practice."

Also, know where you are riding. Remember to observe all mountain rules. Each one is a bit different. Know the posted signs, the out-of-bounds markers and don't go where you are not supposed to go.

In many areas today, snowboarders and skiers share the slopes. This can sometimes pose a problem since skiers still tend to go top to bottom along the fall line of the hill, while snowboarders often carve side-to-side in looping, S-shaped curves. Because snowboarders also are strapped to their boards at an angle, they have something of a blind spot as they carve. A rider is either facing one side of the slope or the other. On his toe side he can see people coming down the hill. But on the heel side, or the backside, he can't see anyone behind him. A reckless snowboarder making a sharp heel-side turn can easily collide with a skier coming straight down the hill. So be extra careful when sharing the slopes with skiers.

Some other general rules for safe snowboarding: If you are coming up behind or are about to pass another rider—snowboarder *or* skier—try to let them know you are there. You can do this by simply shouting, "Coming up on your right!" or "Coming up on your left!" This will often stop them from making a sudden turn and hitting you.

Don't be a wiseguy and cut closely across the path of another rider, figuring you can just make it. Sometimes you won't. Don't ever block a narrow trail or path that is used regularly. If you stop for any reason, get off the trail quickly. Should you fall, try to get up and out of the way as fast as you can.

Also, never stop just below the crest of a hill. Oncoming riders approaching the crest will not see you there. Don't try new, reckless, or dangerous stunts in heavy-traffic areas, especially if the slope is shared by both skiers and fellow snowboarders. Never bump, push, or clown around with another rider who might not be expecting it. There is a place for that kind of roughhouse riding. It's called boarder-cross and will be discussed in a later chapter.

Many people ask about the chance of injury in snowboarding. A logical question is whether the sport is more or less dangerous than skiing; everyone who watches Alpine events has seen some bad falls. The consensus seems to be that snowboarding is the safer sport, though that doesn't mean a rider can't suffer an injury.

Snowboarder/photographer Shawn Frederick is one who feels snowboarding is safer, but he also qualifies his opinion:

"In snowboarding, your feet are strapped into one element," Frederick says. "I've seen skis pop off and hit someone right in the face. This rarely happens with a snowboard. Just carving downhill or racing the slalom, snowboarders are less likely to suffer leg or knee injuries than are skiers. So I think snowboarding is a little safer unless you're riding the halfpipe. That's a different story."

Freestyle snowboarding champion Don Szabo agrees that snowboarders are not as vulnerable to leg and knee injuries as skiers, but feels the upper body is more likely to be injured on the single board.

"I've known people who have broken wrists, elbows, and shoulders," Szabo says. "I've dislocated my shoulder, in fact, on a big jump. I just kind of fell forward and dug my arm in the snow and my body rolled over it. I think because your feet are tied onto the same board you can't really kick a leg out when you start to fall. That leaves the upper body exposed. Skiers tend to kick a leg out and it's the leg that gets hurt."

But other opinions vary. Freestyle champion Shannon Dunn thinks the chance of injury is the same in both sports. She says she never got hurt while learning to snowboard. "I had a slight wrist injury one time," she says, "but mostly I fell on my butt or my knees. My knees would get a little sore, but that's all. But I did have a friend who hurt a leg snowboarding and another who hurt a leg skiing."

Because snowboarding is still a relatively new sport in terms of large numbers of participants, there really hasn't been enough time for a complete study of injuries and the likelihood of their occurrence. But as with any sport that involves speed, maneuverability, races, obstacles, and stunts, there is always the chance of injury. The next several sections of this book hopefully will encourage new snowboarders to participate in the sport, and to increase their skills and avoid injury.

FITNESS AND TRAINING

To think you can go up and snowboard without any degree of physical fitness is simply wrong. You might be able to learn the basics without any ill effects except some sore muscles. But once you begin to take the sport seriously you must have a solid degree of fitness in both the upper and lower body.

"The majority of the strength needed to snowboard comes from your lower body," explains Shawn Frederick. "However, in freestyle riding, the most popular discipline today, an overall level of fitness is needed. That's because of the twisting and turning involved in the tricks. So while the majority of the effort comes from the legs, to be physically fit throughout is important. Balance and flexibility are also key ingredients to overall snowboarding success."

There are two roads to general snowboarding fitness. The first is to prepare your body through a serious of conditioning exercises and stretching. The second is to cross-train—to participate in a number of sports either directly or indirectly related to snowboarding.

The first step, especially for someone who has not been active in sports, is to achieve a solid degree of aerobic fitness. Simply put, aerobic exercise helps to condition the cardiovascular system—the heart and lungs—by increasing the body's efficient intake of oxygen. Good aerobic fitness will allow you to snowboard for an entire afternoon without getting tired.

Aerobic fitness can be achieved in a number of ways. Running is probably the most basic exercise that comes to mind. But jumping rope, riding a bicycle, jazz dancing, or any discipline that raises the level of your heartbeat can help you achieve aerobic fitness. To increase endurance, any aerobic exercise should be done for twenty to thirty minutes, at least three or four times a week. By elevating your heart rate nonstop for this amount of time, you will become more fit to participate in snowboarding or, for that matter, any other sport.

A word of caution. If you decide to run, invest in a good pair of running shoes. They will protect your feet and joints. Also be sure to warm up with a set program of stretching exercises. And when you finish, you can cool down by once again going through the same stretching routine. A good stretching program will also give you added flexibility, an all-important ingredient in freestyle snowboarding.

Stretching exercises should always be done slowly and smoothly, without quick, herky-jerky motions. Hold the maximum point of the stretch for fifteen to twenty seconds, or longer. You will feel the muscle stretching, but you should not feel pain or discomfort. If the stretch is painful, release it slowly. Stretching not only gives the muscles more flexibility, but also makes them less likely to pull or tear during participation in any physical activity or sport.

Before getting into specific stretching exercises, a quick word on additional exercises. Besides stretching and aerobics, general fitness will be improved by regularly engaging in old standbys such as sit-ups, push-ups, and pull-ups. Strong abdominal muscles help support the lower back, which is under some strain while snowboarding. Push-ups and pull-ups will strengthen the arms and shoulders, an important part of training for freestyle and halfpipe riding.

A supervised program of weight training is another way to get in shape and keep in shape. Go to a qualified instructor and tell him which sports you'll be doing. He can suggest the proper exercises for you. As a rule, light weights and high repetitions will serve you best. Heavy weights are designed more for simply putting on muscle mass. With snowboarding, flexibility is the key.

Now, back to stretching. Snowboarders should concentrate on the legs and lower back. Stretching out the hamstring muscle is a good starting point. The hamstring is the large muscle that runs down the back of the leg at the thigh. One of the best and easiest ways to stretch it is to stand before a rail or bench that is about waist-high. Place one leg on the support, keeping it straight. You can bend the other leg at the knee very slightly.

Start the stretch by leaning forward at the waist and sliding your hands down the outstretched leg toward your foot. As your hands get closer to your foot you'll begin to feel the hamstring stretch. Go as far as you can without pain or discomfort and then hold the stretch for fifteen to twenty seconds. Then straighten up slowly. Next, switch legs and stretch your other hamstring. Both legs can be stretched, alternately, five or more times.

Another basic exercise that will stretch not only the hamstring but the lower-back muscles as well is called the *hurdler's stretch*. This is done by sitting on the ground or floor with your legs spread apart and in front of you. One leg is then folded back, bent at the knee, and tucked tight to the buttocks. To do the stretch, bend forward from the waist and move your hands down the outstretched leg. Again, go as far as you can without pain and hold the position for the allotted time. Then repeat with the other leg and alternate, five times each.

To continue working the lower-back muscles, lie down on your back on a flat surface. Then bend one leg at the knee and put your hands around your thigh just above the knee. Pull the leg up as tight to your stomach as you can. Hold for twenty seconds and then repeat with the other leg. You should feel the stretching of the lower-back muscles with this one.

The quadriceps (front thigh muscles) or *quads* can be stretched by holding a wall, rail or even a chair for balance. Then raise one foot behind you, bending it at the knee, and grab your ankle or lower shin with your hand. Pull your foot back toward the buttocks until you feel the stretching in the quad. Hold again, then release and go to the other leg. Stretch each leg five times.

Stretch the calf muscles by standing two feet or so from a wall. Put your hands on the wall and move both feet back as far as they'll go with both heel and toe still touching the floor. The farther away from the wall you place your feet, the more your calf muscles can stretch. This stretch can be done with both legs simultaneously or one leg at a time. Hold and repeat.

These are just a few ways to stretch some of the major muscles used in snowboarding. Skiers, skateboarders, and surfers can follow the same routine. A coach, trainer, or even an experienced snowboarder may suggest additional exercises. Stretching is just a great habit for any athlete. Even during the off-season or a couple of off-days, keep stretching. It will pay dividends.

CROSSOVER SPORTS

In most cases, the best way to learn a sport is to participate, practice, and compete. Then practice some more. Snowboarding is one of the few sports where both beginners and even experienced riders can benefit from cross-training. For example, snowboarders who have come over from skiing, skateboarding, or surfing have generally picked up snowboarding faster than a beginner who has never been involved in the other sports.

Conversely, snowboarders have their choice of several sports that will help sharpen their skills or just keep them in good riding condition. Some can be used as training tools even when the mountain and the snow are available. Others are excellent methods to get ready and even improve for the following season when there is no snow to ride.

Skiing is not really considered a cross-training tool. Skiers who come over to snowboarding rarely go back. After all, both sports take place on the mountain, so if there's a choice, the rider picks up his snowboard, not a pair of skis.

Skateboarding is another story. In fact, snowboarding competition in the halfpipe comes directly from skateboarding. Even the tricks are the same, most of them copied directly from skateboarding. This has helped a number of top snowboarders. Like Shannon Dunn, they find doing these same tricks even easier on a snowboard.

"In skateboarding, if you do one thing wrong you're off the board," Dunn explains. "It's hard to stay on it because there are no bindings. So with snowboarding, you have a lot more to play with. It's easier with a long board [the snowboard vs. the skateboard] because you have more stability. It's pretty easy to control. Skateboarding is definitely much harder."

Shannon Melhuse, one of the top Alpine racers today, started his snowboarding career as a freestyler. He attributes that to skateboarding.

"I had done a lot of halfpipe on skateboards," Melhuse says, "so that made it easier at the beginning because the technique is very similar. But then I slowly got away from it because racing became a stronger discipline for me. But that doesn't mean I won't get back into it someday."

Don Szabo, another former skateboarder, says that one skill doesn't automatically follow the other. "I have friends who can't skateboard at all who have picked up snowboarding very quickly. At the same time, I've had skateboarding friends who just didn't pick up snowboarding quickly."

The largest benefit of skateboarding is definitely in the halfpipe. Body control, flexibility, and board-grabs all come from skating. If you already know how to skateboard and also compete in snowboarding halfpipe, then the skating experience can continue to be beneficial. If you pick up snowboarding from scratch and go into the pipe, you might be better off just staying there. Trying to pick up skateboarding (which has no bindings) as a secondary sport might not be as beneficial, though there are some snowboarders who will still recommend it. Basically, it's your choice.

Surfing is a more interesting story. Though there are no bindings used on a surfboard, the movements and the feeling of the sport are very close to snowboarding.

"You're seeing many snowboarders today turning into surfers," says Rick

Waring. "There is a real parallel between surf and snow as far as the thrill factor is concerned. Craig Kelly, one of the great snowboarders of all time, is sixty-percent surfer now."

Don Szabo is another who sees surfing as an excellent crossover sport for snowboarders. "Snowboarding is definitely more like surfing than skate-boarding," he says. "On a skateboard, you just have to lean when you want to turn. The trucks do the turning for you. Turning on a surfboard is almost identical to the snowboard. You have to shift your weight in the same way."

So if you live in a warm-weather climate and have a long off-season from snowboarding, surfing will be a great crossover sport. It will improve your balance, enable you to retain your condition and flexibility, and even give you a chance to work on some techniques that you can transfer back to the mountain when the next snow season comes along.

Here's a cross-training tool that might surprise some new snowboarders. Working on a trampoline is a great way to improve your freestyle snow-boarding techniques. Shannon Dunn is part of a group of pros who have given snowboarding demonstrations on the East Coast during the summer. How did they do it with no snow?

"We just set up a trampoline and jump on it with our boards. We can do tricks and different grabs that you do in the halfpipe. But it isn't only used for demos. A lot of halfpipe riders use the trampoline in the summer to work on their grabs."

Craig Kelly has called the trampoline "air awareness." Jumping on a tramp' with your board will help you improve your balance skills on the board. It will help you get used to the feel of the board in midair. And while you can't get as high off the surface on a trampoline, it's a great way to practice body flexibility in making halfpipe grabs.

If you decide to use a tramp' for cross-training, just make sure it's protected from any sharp edges on your board or bindings. If there are

11 JIMMY HALOPOFF AT A TRAMPOLINE DEMONSTRATION IN SOUTHERN CALIFORNIA.

burrs or sharp metal edges from riding rocks the previous season, file them down. Then, happy jumping.

Many snowboarders are beginning to go mountain biking during the off-season. Biking on the roads is great aerobic exercise. Mountain biking is too, but it also adds something else. Riding over rough and unknown terrain enables the biker to develop upper-body balance skills. He must also look ahead and pick a line over which to ride, something he must also do on his snowboard.

Zipping down a hill on a mountain bike can almost resemble a slalom course, and it often emulates an obstacle course as well. In fact, one article on cross-training went as far as to say that "mountain biking is snowboarding, or as close as you'll get without a board of some kind."

Many snowboarders have also taken up in-line skating as a cross-training tool during the off-season or between trips to the mountain. In-line skating, in a sense, has elements of both snowboarding and skiing, so skiers use it for the same reason. The form and posture of an in-line skater is similar to that of the snowboarder. That's one advantage.

Being aware of the fall line and unweighting out of turns is something else board riders must do as second nature, and in-line skating helps make them aware of this. In addition, skating is an aerobic exercise for general conditioning and works some important muscle groups, including the ones that keep a rider centered over his board.

So, overall fitness and training is important for both the newcomer and the experienced snowboarder. Getting into condition is the first step. Staying in shape all year round comes next. Then, finding some cross-training tools so you can work on snowboarding techniques whenever you want is the next thing an avid snowboarder should do. The advice, exercises, and techniques that have been discussed in this chapter are a great starting point for anyone.

PART THREE

CHRISTIE ELDER ENJOYING A FREERIDING DAY IN COLORADO.

LEARNING TO SNOWBOARD

THE BASICS—RIDING, TURNING, STOPPING

ONCE you have the proper board, bindings, boots, and clothing, you're finally ready to go. If you have been a skier, skateboarder, or surfer you will probably have an advantage as a beginning snowboarder. But for those who have no crossover experience and are getting up on a snowboard for the first time, here goes:

One thing you will have to know before you get on the board for the first time is which foot you feel most comfortable having in front. Most boarders use the *regular-foot* method, with their left foot in the front binding. But some prefer putting their right foot up front. While this is called *goofy foot* (another term from skateboarding), there is really nothing wrong with it. It's almost like being right-handed or left-handed. The difference here is that the bindings will have to be turned to accommodate the goofy-foot rider.

Also, make sure that someone shows you how to properly secure the bindings, so they are not too loose or too tight. Now you're ready for your

12   HOW TO BUCKLE INTO
     PLATE BINDINGS.

HOW TO STRAP IN FREESTYLE
BINDINGS.   13

first trip down a hill—not a mountain, just a hill. But you do have to pick one where there is a little slope. You can't learn to snowboard on a flat surface or when you are barely moving.

There are some people who try to learn to snowboard as they would learn to ski. This doesn't work. New skiers can go as slow as one mile an hour and never fall because they can spread their feet at any time to keep their stability. Snowboarders can't do this because their feet are strapped into a single board.

The first time on the board the tendency is to lean forward or backward, and if you're moving at a crawl, you may just fall over. You certainly won't get hurt. It's just a matter of losing your balance. So the key to learning is to work up the courage to pick up some speed and move a little faster. The momentum you will pick up moving down the hill will actually stop you from falling over and will give you a better feel for the board and the edges.

If you have to push your way to the hill or even push to get up a little speed, there is a way to do it. Unclip the straps on your back binding only and then just push the snowboard with your back foot over the flat area. By doing this, you can glide on the snowboard much the way someone pushes and glides with a skateboard. This is another way to get used to moving on the board. An experienced rider can reach down and buckle his binding without stopping. But when the newcomer reaches the hill, he will have to stop gliding and secure his back binding once again.

Now, practice riding straight down a hill with enough slope to give you that speed. The important thing here is body posture. Be sure to get in the right position for riding the hill. The natural tendency is to bend at the waist toward the slope of the hill while keeping the legs straight. This is incorrect. Instead, bend up and down at the knees, using them as shock absorbers. Keep your body and shoulders directly over the middle of the board. And most importantly, keep your knees together.

14   HOW TO SKATE ON FLAT AREAS.

Your feet will be about eighteen or nineteen inches apart in the bindings. By bending at the knees and keeping them together, you're creating an angle between your legs. It may seem awkward at first, but if you look at any good snowboarder coming down a hill, his knees are always held together.

This is the basic position for gliding down a hill. Once you can do this comfortably, with your knees bent and held together, and with your weight over the board, then you're ready to work on controlling your speed. And this is done by going from edge to edge—by turning.

An experienced snowboarder can control his speed every time he turns. Sometimes a rider will be coming down the mountain making beautiful looping turns, with the powdered snow cascading back from his edges. It's a beautiful sight, but in reality the rider is often just making the turns to check his speed so he doesn't build up too much forward momentum.

To learn the technique of turning, the new rider must be able to generate some speed. That's another reason step one is to glide down a hill at moderate speed. If you're going too slowly, you won't turn, you'll just fall over. So, before trying to turn, you must begin to ride straight down a hill, assuming the correct posture and picking up speed. If your weight is centered correctly, the entire base of the board will be in contact with the snow surface.

Turning technique begins with the upper body. Everything else follows in sequence. In other words, where your shoulders go, your waist will follow. And where your waist goes, your feet will go. This is the basic principle. Now, let's see how it's done.

If you're a regular-foot rider with your left foot forward, you would begin a *frontside* or right-hand turn by dropping your right shoulder and rolling your left shoulder across the top of the board. You can help this movement by also bringing your left arm over. Once you do this, your left hip will almost automatically follow.

15

16

17

With the knees properly bent, this movement of arm, shoulder, and hip will shift your weight from the center to the inside edge and back part of the board. The board will make a turn to the right. Remember, the proper weight shift will keep the edge on the front part of the board from digging in. If that happens, the board will not turn properly.

To come out of a turn you simply square up your body and shift your weight back to the center of the board. That will bring the board off the edge and out of the turn. You will now be traveling in the direction you have turned. Next, you should try a left-hand or *backside* turn. This one is a little more difficult, though the technique is basically the same.

Start by dropping your left shoulder toward the snow and roll your right arm and shoulder across the top of the board. Again this will cause the right hip to follow and thus shift your weight to the left and rear. Once again your left edge, from the middle to the rear of the board, will dig in and cause the board to turn. To bring it straight, just square up and return your weight to the center of the board.

Turning is not difficult once you master the weight shift. But just listen to how Shawn Frederick describes turning. This is something that can't be taught. It must be felt.

"Turning must be done with a real light finesse touch," Frederick says. "You're dealing with snow and a stainless steel edge, so you don't have to put a lot of power into it. Don't put all your weight on the edge and dig it in. If you do that, you'll stick an edge and fall, or the edge will be buried too deep to get out and you'll stay in the turn.

"It's a gradual motion done smoothly. The smoother you are, the more relaxed you are, the better off you'll be and the quicker you'll become proficient at turning the board."

Beginners going down a long hill should make turns at about a 70-degree angle. A 90-degree turn would take you directly out to the side and slow you down too much. A 45-degree turn on a moderately steep slope wouldn't slow you down enough. You'd find yourself going too fast for your skill level. A 70-degree turn will keep the speed constant and controllable, allowing you to practice toe-side and heel-side turns, one after the other, all the way down the hill. However, if a new rider feels he is still going too fast, he can make one or two 90-degree turns to slow to the desired speed.

Making big turns across the run is the best way to learn. Sometimes you'll be traveling parallel to the mountain. Small turns simply won't give a new rider a good feel of the board. Small 45-degree turns on a moderate slope might speed you up to twenty-five or thirty miles an hour. That's too fast for a beginner. You've got to find a happy medium because you don't want to go too fast when you're learning, or too slow, either.

Turning is one of the keys to snowboarding fun. It's a skill that must be learned early and then perfected. Whether you wind up as a slalom racer or a freestyler, the ability to turn your board right and left is indispensable.

Stopping is not nearly as important a skill in snowboarding as it is in other sports. The snowboarder is usually going to travel from point A to point B and won't worry about stopping in between. If there is an obstacle such as a tree or rock, the rider will either go around it or jump over it.

But for beginners, there are a couple of ways to stop the board if it's absolutely necessary. At slow speeds, the easiest way is to simply sit down. Just like that. Relax and sit. You may slide a little, but both rider and board will eventually stop.

The second basic way to stop is with a radical turn. As we already explained, turning is a way to control speed and slow the board. Therefore, if you make a turn of more than 90 degrees, you'll actually start up the mountain again and come to a stop. If you want to stop quickly, just use the technique for turning. As your board turns, start digging the edge in deeper by putting more pressure on your back foot. The tail of the board

18

19

20

21 HOW TO MAKE THE HEEL SIDE FALL PROPERLY.

22 THE BEST ADVICE: DON'T PANIC!

will slide around and, as the edge continues to dig deeper into the snow, it will stop the board.

In a sense, that's almost like a stop on ice in hockey. Some experienced riders can use the hockey-stop. As they're headed straight in one direction, they will almost make a little hop-turn to throw the board sideways. Then they'll put pressure on the rear edge of the board and come to a skidding stop.

This is similar to a maneuver called the *sideslip*. The sideslip is often used by experienced riders, to slow them down on a real steep grade or narrow vertical chute. With the sideslip, the board is parallel to the slope of the hill and the rider is actually going down sideways, toe-side in front. He controls his speed by putting his weight on the heel-side, the edge facing back up the mountain. The front edge of the board will actually come out of the snow by perhaps three or four inches. He controls his movement by his weight and if he wants to stop, can simply dig down harder with the heel-side until the board ceases to move.

One quick word about falling off your snowboard: Because your feet are in the bindings at an angle, you'll usually fall to one side or the other. Unless you're a hotdogger doing some wild freestyle stunts or flips, you won't fall head over heels down the mountain.

But if you start to fall to the heel-side, simply sit down and slide to a stop on your buttocks. You may be a little sore, but you shouldn't get hurt. If you fall to the toe-side, then you've got to try to cushion the fall with your hands or forearms and then slide to a stop. Again, if the snow is soft, chances of injury are slim.

These are the basics. They aren't difficult to learn and before long you'll be carving your own path down the mountain, controlling your speed with large, graceful turns, and enjoying a sport that gets into your blood and generally stays. Now it's time to look ahead and see what you can do about entering some of the competitive disciplines, or the out-of-bounds world of the freestyler.

Monty Roach showing style with his frontside nose-bone at A-Basin, Colorado.

Quite possibly the world's most recognized professional snowboarder, Craig Kelly, showing why he won four world championships with this huge backside method air.

Jimmy Halopoff showing why he's one of the world's best freestylers with this reverse Walt-air over a cornice.

Keith "Duck Boy" Wallace, one of the best with contorting and tricks.

Jimmy Halopoff, over the edge.

Jimmi Scott electrifies the crowds at Eldora Mountain, Colorado.

J. D. Platt, who has been seen on billboards and in magazines all over the United States, explodes the top of a cornice in Bend, Oregon, only to find a double overhead freefall drop.

Jimmy Halopoff shows textbook control as he hurls himself over the edge.

Loveland Pass, Colorado, is the premier spot for deep powder, huge cornices, and guys like Jimmy Halopoff.

World–class halfpipe contender Crystal Aldana shows that not only the men have what it takes to succeed. Here she's illustrating a chicken salad.

Jimmi Scott showing that he too is a master of seven-foot aerials.

Jimmy Halopoff has time for a wave to the camera as he flies six feet out of the halfpipe.

1992 United States Alpine Champion Shannon Melhuse on his winning run at the Mount Bachelor, Oregon, Championships.

While Rob Morrow (left) is maintaining his composure, his teammate Noah Brandon has different ideas of flying over cornices.

Goofy-footer Nick Calovito of New York and four-time World Champion Terry Kidwell of Northern California deal with one of the three drops they'll face in this run down the giant slalom course.

ADVANCED DISCIPLINES

ALPINE RACING

ALPINE racing on a snowboard has evolved directly from skiing, where the slalom events have been contested by many competitors from many countries for years. Alpine racing on skis is also one of the glamour events of the Winter Olympics. With many former skiers taking up snowboarding, it's no surprise that slalom, racing around gates on a downhill course, has also become a major force on the snowboarding scene.

Snowboarders can cover a course in nearly the same time as skiers without the benefit of poles. But they can really move. Shannon Melhuse, who was the World Cup super–giant slalom champion and won the United States Pro Tour title in the giant slalom in 1991–92, talks about his specialty events:

"Riders in the super-giant slalom hit speeds from sixty to seventy miles per hour," Melhuse says. "The gates are farther apart, there is more speed and a bigger board. Helmets are also required. This race is really close to the downhill in skiing. It's a lot faster and longer course than the giant slalom.

"In the giant slalom, the riders travel in the thirty to fifty mile-per-hour range, depending on the layout of the course. Competition is getting more intense. Every year there are good new people coming in to challenge the older competitors. The United States seems to have better riders in the super-giant slalom, while the Europeans excel in slalom."

At the World Cup, there are competitions in super-giant slalom, slalom, and halfpipe. The United States tour has giant slalom and the pipe. All three slalom disciplines have similar techniques.

23 TERJE HAKONSON (LEFT) AND JACK COGLAN (RIGHT) SIDE BY SIDE ON THE GIANT SLALOM COURSE AT A-BASIN, COLORADO.

With the giant slalom, there are about thirty-seven gates used in the championships. Courses vary somewhat, but the usual time for a top-notch rider to finish the course is between 1:00 and 1:05. The distance varies between the gates. The giant-slalom course is not symmetrical, some of the turns having a tighter apex than others.

The giant-slalom course follows the contour of the mountain, crossing the fall line in several places. By contrast, the slalom course is completely symmetrical and follows the fall line of the hill. Gates are close together and turns must be made quickly. This is the shortest of the three slalom races. But some competitors, like Chris Karol, love it and hope it becomes part of the U.S. tour.

"Racing is so intense because it's just an all-out adrenaline rush," Karol once said. "Thirty seconds where nothing else in the world matters except the gates in front of you. Full speed. You have no time to think, just react."

Another top racer, Mike Kildevaeld, feels the slalom races very closely mirror the ski races they evolved from. He should know, since he is a former state high-school Alpine ski champion. Now, snowboarding is his thing.

"The only difference between snowboard racing and ski racing is that we don't have poles and we can't straddle gates," Kildevaeld said. "Otherwise, it's all the same."

The techniques for going around the various gates of a slalom or giant-slalom course are basically the same as for turning. Only the speed is greater, the turns sharper, and the idea is to not slow down. A racer also has to be thinking one gate ahead. How he sets up to cut a gate depends on the placement of the next gate. That will dictate how sharp his turn will be, how wide he will have to swing, and how close to the gate he should be.

When you make a sharp turn on a slalom course, you must lean much more than you do with a lazy turn on a slope. More of your weight is

24 WORLD CUP ALPINE CONTENDER CHRIS KAROL DEMONSTRATES THE PROPER TECHNIQUE FOR APPROACHING HEEL-SIDE TURNS.

forward and the outside edge of the board will leave the snow surface because you're digging so hard on the inside edge. That's called *setting the edge*. On a smaller turn, the kind you make in the slalom, you don't have to set the edge as hard and consequently don't need as much of a lean.

United States Alpine racers are very serious about their sport. Eric Webster, who has been racing since 1985, states his ambition very frankly: "I want to be the best American slalom racer," he said. To keep in shape, Webster runs thirty miles a week and spends a lot of time mountain biking near his home in New Hampshire. He also admires the European racers.

"European ski-training tradition has carried over to their snowboarders," he said. "The racers are well supported and well disciplined. I want to be in that atmosphere, so I'm going to try to race with them."

It's very difficult to tell a beginner how to become a slalom or giant-slalom racer. The obvious way is to watch some racers in action. Observe their techniques, the way they take the gates, come out of their turns, and get ready for the next gate. Set up a gate or two on a moderately sloped hill and try cutting them slowly. Some tips and advice from a racer or certified instructor will also help.

After you do this for a while, you must decide how far you want to go as a competitive racer. If you feel you are serious about it, sign up with a team and train with them. Then try some races on the amateur circuit. The USASA (United States Amateur Snowboard Association) has its own league and its own instructors. They run strictly Alpine events, no halfpipe.

Most of the courses on the amateur circuit are not laid out on steep hills and they don't have that many gates. They give the rider a chance to run gates on a fairly easy course. It's a good way to get experience and to see if you are cut out for Alpine racing. To get better at the slalom races takes a world of practice. Betsy Shaw, who converted to snowboarding after being a skiing star with the University of New Hampshire ski team, said that experience in the gates is the only way to go.

"Training hard in the gates makes all the difference in the world," said Shaw. "You can go out freeriding for as long as you want, but it won't make you better in a race."

Alpine racing on snowboards is rapidly growing in the United States, Europe, and Japan. There are many more competitors and more television coverage. There's a good chance that these will be the first snowboarding events to get into the Olympics.

A beginner looking to become an Alpine racer is facing a lot of hard work and practice. It won't happen overnight. But if competitive racing is your thing and you are willing to pay the practice price, then by all means, go for it.

THE HALFPIPE

Riding the halfpipe is a discipline that comes directly from skateboarding. Because of this, many of the first halfpipe riders were former skateboarders. In some ways, it was easy for them to convert. They already knew the tricks and the rhythm of the sport. And going from a skateboard, which has no bindings, to a snowboard with bindings made them feel loose and relaxed. There was no way to go off the board.

Oddly enough, many Alpine racers have no real feel for the halfpipe. Top racer Chris Karol looks at the pipe this way:

"I was at the first halfpipe contest ever, in Soda Springs, California, and it was a joke," Karol said. "It was more like a bunch of mounds that people jumped off. It was weak, and it's still like that now."

That's a pretty radical view, but it points out just how different the two disciplines are. Betsy Shaw, another top Alpine racer, has a more modified view of the pipe.

"I like riding in halfpipes," she said, "but I don't like competing in them. Halfpipe contests are like putting on a show and I don't like to be a performer. But I love the rhythm of a slalom course. The speed and rhythm combined with the feel of carving is great."

You get a contrasting opinion from Shannon Dunn. She started as a skier, found herself burnt out, and didn't like competition. When she started snowboarding, she soon began gravitating toward the halfpipe.

"I really went more into freestyle when I starting snowboarding," she says. "Lots of freeriding. Then I got into the pipe the same year I started and a year later I began competing. I just liked the pipe a lot right from the start. There was nothing about skiing that was as much fun and I was never really into racing.

"The halfpipe is a different kind of competitiveness. You just have so much more freedom. To me, it's almost not like a competition at all because you do your own thing."

Don Szabo is a rider who came directly from skateboarding. It's not surprising that he enjoys competing in the halfpipe because he did many of the same things on skateboard ramps. Yet his first taste of snowboarding wasn't in the pipe. It was on the mountain.

"I still remember the first run I took on a snowboard," Szabo recalls. "It was a great experience, the rush going down the mountain, the wind in your face, making turns and being able to go anywhere you want. A real downhill."

But gradually Don Szabo moved to freestyling. He loves both the obstacle courses and the halfpipe. But he does admit that the pipe is not natural to the sport.

"The halfpipe is really a takeoff on skateboarding," says Szabo. "It was created because it can be contained really well for judging and public demonstration. It's a lot of fun, even though it isn't 'natural' snowboarding. There are kids now who grew up riding the halfpipes and that's all they think. Halfpipe."

Before going any further into halfpipe riding it's time for a word of caution. It's based on the final thing that Don Szabo said: Kids only know halfpipe. Szabo feels they should know more.

"These kids don't think about where snowboarding really came from, that it's going out and riding with your friends and riding over all the natural terrain."

There is a trap for those who are interested in the halfpipe and nothing else. They miss some of the other great fun of snowboarding, and in some cases, lack the skills to go out and carve a mountain or run an obstacle course.

"Halfpipe riders should definitely know how to snowboard," says Shannon Dunn. "I've seen some riders who hardly know the basics of riding

25 TYPICAL FREESTYLE HALFPIPE, ELDORA MOUNTAIN, COLORADO.

and they're already in the pipe. I can't believe they're trying it so soon and it usually doesn't look as if they're having much fun. You've got to learn to snowboard, get your balance. Otherwise, the pipe is tough and newcomers wonder why they can't do it. So I tell everyone, you've got to know how to ride the board first."

The halfpipe is a long chute with a downward slope, the shape resembling a big pipe that's been cut in half. It is built up on each side with a snow ramp, allowing the rider to go up one side, do a trick (called a *hit*), then come down and go back up the other side for another maneuver; all the while he is working his way through the pipe. The early pipes were sometimes just rough mounds of snow. Now they are constructed with more precision, are more uniform, and there are more of them.

Rick Waring, executive director of the U.S. Snowboarding Tour, knows firsthand how interest in the halfpipe has grown.

"We get calls every day from people who want to know about halfpipes and ask us to send them specs and dimensions. Sometimes they'll ask if there is someone who can come out and help them build one. In the last year or so, many resorts are beginning to build halfpipes as part of their recreation facilities."

Waring also feels that someone who wants to learn the halfpipe on a snowboard should skateboard as well. "It's a natural crossover," he says. "It has a lot to do with balance, so if you want to compete in the pipe you should skateboard, especially if there is no snow all year round. With a skateboard, you can practice any time."

What about someone who has some basic snowboarding skills and wants to start learning the pipe? Shannon Dunn learned at first by watching, then got some help from her brother. She also watched videos, but ultimately it was a matter of "just going out and doing it."

Don Szabo suggests that newcomers to the pipe start slowly, though he was somewhat self-taught.

"I had a skateboarding background and more or less learned myself. Now it's easier to get some instruction at a snowboarding camp or at a resort. Basically, a newcomer should just get in there and get the feel of the pipe. Work it back and forth until you get a sense of your edges. Don't think about aerials or about grabbing the board. First learn to work your way back and forth and up and down the sides."

Shannon Dunn agrees. Step one is to learn to work the pipe and the walls. "Just get in there and carve the walls," she says. "Slowly work your way higher and higher. Get the feel of going up and down and try to be as smooth as you can. Eventually, you reach the point where you can get air. But don't rush it. It took me a long time to become smooth and the people who are the smoothest work their way up faster."

A newcomer to the pipe must learn the basic turn right away. You can't go up one side of the pipe unless you know how to turn and come back down. If you are going up the wall while facing down the pipe, that is called the *frontside wall*. Because you unweight (shift your weight up and forward) as you start up the wall, the board will be on the toe-edge. Turn your head and shoulders back toward the bottom of the pipe and your body will follow. You can then shift your weight back and pivot or almost make a little hop-turn with the board. It's a technique you can also practice on the ground.

Going up the *backside wall* (your body facing where you started the pipe), the technique is almost the same. Turn your head and shoulders into the turn, shift your weight back and pivot the tail end of the board. You can pivot the tail or do a little hop-turn.

To simply ride the walls of the pipe, keep your body low (bent at the knees) and centered over the board. Staying low keeps your weight centered and makes your ride smoother. You kind of pump up the walls much as you do in skateboarding. Riders will get real low as they come down one side, then quickly unweight during the transition, straightening their legs and shifting their weight from the rear to the front as they go up the wall. So it's really a matter of learning to weight and unweight quickly and efficiently.

After a new rider can work the pipe, go from wall to wall smoothly, and reach the top with no problem, then he is ready to *catch air*. That's the first step to becoming a halfpipe competitor. Once a rider is in the air, there's no limit to the number of tricks and stunts he can do.

Don Szabo has maintained that snowboard halfpipe is an imitative sport. It's so much like skateboarding that snowboarders always grab their board during aerials even though their feet are strapped in with bindings. Skateboarders grab the board to keep it from falling away and to keep themselves from wiping out. While some snowboarding aerials are done without the hand touching the board, the board-grab is part of most of them and probably the best way to learn.

Once you can smoothly reach the top of the wall it's time to go one step further. Work up to the speed you want. After you unweight to start driving up the wall, bend at the knees once again. When the nose of the board is at the top of the wall, flex your knees and unweight with a slight forward lean. This strong movement should take you up and out of the pipe.

The first things you must learn are the simple *frontside air* and *backside air*. These are the simplest ways to turn and return to the pipe. The frontside air is a turn in the direction your feet are facing. If you go up the left wall with your feet facing the end of the pipe you'll make your frontside air to the right.

Once you're in the air, compress your body, bringing your legs up by bending at the knees. Then reach down with your left arm and grab the right side of the board between your feet. This movement will begin the body pivot that will result in a turn. Follow the grab by quickly pivoting your hips and shoulders to the right, in the direction of the turn.

As you feel the board turning and beginning to return to the surface, release the grab and extend your legs. As you land, bend at the knees once more and ride the board down. Now you are in position to pump and unweight, which will drive you up the other side of the wall.

The backside air is just the opposite, but with a slight variation. This time you'll be turning right but with your feet pointing left. As you come out of the pipe you don't reach across your body. Instead, reach down with the right hand and grab the board up closer to the nose. Then pivot your body—head, shoulders, and hips—to the right. The landing and trip back down the pipe is the same as with the frontside air.

Practice these two basic aerials until you are totally comfortable with them and can do them with ease, working the pipe from side to side. From there, you can begin to perfect your own halfpipe routine. Then you'll be ready to compete.

• • •

Following are a group of sample aerials that are basic to halfpipe routines. Don't try these until you truly feel you are ready. Watch experienced halfpipe riders do them. Learn their techniques, how they handle the board, and coordinate their body movements. Keep practicing the basics and slowly build on them. Doing it step by step will keep your confidence at a high level and also lessen the chance of injury.

Many of the aerials are named by the way the grab is made. For example, there are a number of frontside aerials that are very similar to one another; there is just a slight variation in style. If you grab the board with your front hand (the hand closest to the nose of the board) on the toe-side of the board and bone out (straighten at the knee) your front leg, the aerial is called a *melancholy*. If you grab the board between your legs on the heelside with your front hand and with your leg boned out, it's called a *chicken salad.*

When you reach down with your back hand in between your heels and bone out your back foot, the air is called a *stalefish.* If you do the same thing but make it a backside turn, then it's a *freshfish.* On both these aerials, boning out the back foot will thrust the board out also, turning the rider sideways in the air before landing back on the surface.

Another turn is called an *indy.* On this one you simply grab the board between your toes with your back hand and bone out your front foot. A frontside air with both legs boned out straight is appropriately called a *stiffie air.* Each of these turns is different in the way the rider contorts his body and where he grabs the board. The style with which he does them is taken into consideration by the judges during a contest.

There are many other tricks a pipe rider can do. Many riders like to do spins in the air, going as far as 540s (one and a half 360-degree turns) and 720s (two 360-degree turns). It takes a lot of practice to do these. "It's difficult to get that rotation, keep it under control and grab the board," said Don Szabo. "In fact, sometimes you can get more of a spin without grabbing the board."

26   1991 AND 1992 WORLD HALFPIPE CHAMPION JEFF BRUSHIE DOING A HUGE
FRONTSIDE LIENAIR AT ELDORA MOUNTAIN, COLORADO.

If you do a frontside turn by coming back down to the surface backward, that's called an *air-to-fakie.* From there, you turn from the fakie, doing a *half-cab,* and come down the pipe facing forward once again.

Halfpipe contests do not allow flips or inverted aerials, such as the McTwist, one of the most spectacular tricks in skateboarding. The only way a rider can do an inverted aerial is if he plants one hand on the rim, or top, of the pipe. These handplant aerials are also similar to skateboarding. Riders must have good upper-body strength and gymnastic ability to do these.

Using a handplant is the only way the board is allowed to extend straight up in the air. Otherwise, it can only turn out to the side. These stunts are difficult and take a lot of practice. Watch the experts, get some tips, then practice handplants without a board. Once you can do a handplant, then it's time to try one in the pipe.

Most competitors in the pipe will all do the same or very similar tricks. Once again, almost all of them come from skateboarding, though Don Szabo, for one, says that he can get higher out of the pipe and can do more things on his snowboard than he could when he was skateboarding.

A halfpipe routine is judged on the difficulty of the tricks, the style with which they are done, and the amount of air the competitor catches, as well as overall presentation. A competitor is usually in the pipe from thirty to sixty seconds, depending somewhat on the length of the pipe itself, which varies.

In shorter pipes, the competitor might get a chance to do six tricks, or *hits,* three on each side. But in a longer pipe there might be time for fourteen or fifteen hits. Competitors do not all have to do the same number of hits. Depending on how they work the pipe, some stay in longer than others. But since the pipe is graded downhill, no one can stay in there indefinitely. Natural forces won't allow it.

"Sometimes you have to give up more hits for the size of the aerial,"

Don Szabo says. "The more of a downhill angle you take in the pipe, the more speed you have to go higher. The shorter distance you go from hit to hit, the less speed and height. But you have more hits."

Shannon Dunn says that in most contests there are four halfpipe runs— a quarterfinal, semifinal, then two final runs. Half the competitors are eliminated in each heat. In the finals, they use the best of the two runs. In World Cup competition, the two runs in the finals both count, with a combined score.

There are generally five judges with a series of scores, similar to the judging in figure skating. In many contests, the high and low scores are dropped, and the three others are averaged. Because snowboarding is still a relatively new sport, there are often complaints about uniformity in judging. Now judges are being trained more closely. And as more former competitors become judges, a greater uniformity should come.

As you can see, halfpipe competition is intense. The competitors practice incessantly, trying to develop new tricks and perfect old ones. Shannon Dunn's only concern is that some halfpipers might burn out by not enjoying the other disciplines in snowboarding.

"Most of the pros are good freeriders," she says. "But some of the people who specialize in the pipe just aren't that good on the mountain. They don't spend enough time there. But I think the whole thing of snowboarding is to have fun freeriding. Even if you compete in the pipe, doing a lot of freeriding helps you with your stamina, your balance, and keeps you from getting burnt out. When I really start to miss freeriding I know I'm feeling signs of burnout. That's when I know it's time to go up the mountain."

That seems to be good advice. Even if halfpipe becomes your favorite discipline, try to make snowboarding a complete sport.

• • •

FREESTYLE

Riding the halfpipe is not the only snowboarding discipline that has evolved directly from skateboarding. A wide range of snowboarding activities, coming under the heading of *freestyle riding,* also derives from freestyle and streetstyle skateboarding. This has become so popular an activity that many resorts have set up obstacle courses and other freestyle areas.

In some ways, the snowboard is a natural for a hotdogging, jumping, and wild kind of freestyle riding. For one thing, the rider is tied to the board with his bindings. That gives him more control than the skateboarder, who might lose his board at any time. The other prime asset of the board is described by snowboarder/photographer Shawn Frederick:

"Because the board has such a springy infrastructure, it makes jumping or doing an *Ollie* relatively easy," Frederick says. "If you kind of lift up on your front foot, you'll feel the tension on the back of the board and you use that to spring up, to do an Ollie. Like skateboarding, it's two very quick movements, done one right after another. Lift the front foot, snap down with the back and up you go."

Because of the bindings, a snowboarder can also go into the air by simply jumping—flexing both knees at the same time, much in the way he would jump off the ground. For freestylers, this leads to many possibilities. They love to Ollie up onto a bench or fallen log and let the board just slide across. Riders keep their weight centered over the board, their hands out in front for balance, and slide. Because they can keep pressure on the board, they maintain good control. And when they start to lose momentum, they simply Ollie or jump off.

While racers and riders with Alpine backgrounds use the manicured slopes to carve their way down a hill, the freestyler is looking for obstacles. He prefers to slide down rails or on logs, jump around moguls (a succession of small hills or bumps) or Ollie over rocks and tree stumps. He prefers a wooded hill to a manicured one.

Here are some of the names for the maneuvers being practiced by free-stylers.

To jump up on an obstacle and slide sideways with the board is called a *basic rail slide* or *wood slide.* To Ollie up and slide with the board straight ahead is called a *50/50.* Some riders will Ollie up and *50/50* across, then go into a *blindside revert.* That means they slide straight down an obstacle, but instead of jumping straight off, they spin in the air, rotating backward toward their blind side. They end up going off the obstacle backward, the revert. Some do another 180 in the air and come down forward. Coming down backward is called a *fakie.* Some riders will then jump in the air, do a 180, and come down facing forward again.

Freestylers also will do a variety of grabs and tricks when they leap off an obstacle or the crest of a hill. The maneuvers are identical to those done

27 JIMMY HALOPOFF ILLUSTRATES A BACKSIDE WOOD SLIDE.

in the halfpipe. So the rider can dismount by doing a *melancholy* or a *chicken salad.* He can combine three or four tricks while mounting and dismounting an obstacle.

Because so many snowboarders began showing a preference for freestyle riding, many resorts and mountain areas have set up obstacle courses. Instead of hauling away fallen trees, they have left them there, creating natural obstacles. What had formerly been out-of-bounds areas of a mountain are now open to freestylers willing to wind their way through the woods. A freestyler will rarely go out on a manicured slope. That kind of riding just isn't his thing. He looks for the challenge, the obstacle, a place to do his tricks.

Many freestylers also come out of that skateboarding background, but they may have been streetstylers who felt too confined in the halfpipe. They would rather do their tricks out in the open, with natural obstacles. In skateboarding, these guys are often considered rebels, outlaw skaters who love to flaunt the rules, and sometimes the law.

But in snowboarding, this kind of riding is perfectly legal. The mountains are catering to the freestylers. Some are even creating areas akin to skateboard parks, with ramps, halfpipes, pools, rails, and obstacle courses. The creation of these areas for freestylers has also brought new converts to snowboarding, crossovers from skateboarding, and even surfing.

So while the halfpipe is highly structured and judged, freestyling is a kind of no-holds-barred form of snowboarding that many riders find perfectly suited to their bold and adventurous tastes. But like any other discipline in the sport, newcomers should hone their skills before flying down an obstacle course. Learn to control your board, to turn well, to slow down, and stop. Then learn to jump and Ollie well before sliding over obstacles.

These days, obstacle courses are being set up for contests, specialty events that take a great deal of skill. Don Szabo, for one, loves this kind of racing.

"The obstacle course is a combination of freestyle and racing," Szabo explains. "Sometimes you run the course for time, sometimes you're judged. I prefer the judged events because it's more of an expression of the way you ride, not just your speed."

Courses contain double and triple jumps that the competitor can roll over one at a time or do a big aerial over all of them. There are banks, *berms* (a kind of ledge), spines (jumps that run parallel to the mountain), as well as gates to go around.

"Snowboarding to me," adds Szabo, "is going down the mountain and dealing with whatever obstacles you come across."

Spoken like a true freestyler. So when you're ready, watch some of the experts. Look at their techniques, how they go from one obstacles to another, one trick to another. Watch the way they time their jumps and their turns. Watch how they soften their landings by bending at the knees, and control their boards by keeping their knees together. You can learn an awful lot by watching. If you have a question, ask it. Then, when you're ready, get out there and rip it up.

PART FOUR

IAN RUHTER, OVER THE TOP OF A WHISTLER, BRITISH COLUMBIA, ROCK CLIFF.

NEW AND RADICAL DISCIPLINES

BOARDER-CROSS

THIS one is strictly for fun. It's relatively new and in a way, it's a lot like a combination of motocross and Roller Derby. It's called *boarder-cross,* and it's an anything-goes race down an obstacle course, by four to eight snowboarders. The objective: First one across the finish line wins.

Boarder-cross is a far cry from any other discipline in snowboarding. It resembles motocross in that the competitors go over a series of jumps and moguls and around corners, much like the motorcycles in motocross. And, like the good ol' Roller Derby, competitors can bump, elbow, and jostle one another on the way down.

In a way, boarder-cross is a natural evolution. As long as people have been competitive, there has been the urge to race. *Beat you to the bottom! Last one there's a rotten egg! Bet I can get there before you!* These kinds of challenges have been repeated over and over again for centuries, whether the competitors are simply running, or are riding skis, bicycles, ice skates, whatever.

Shawn Frederick talks about something called the *Chinese downhill*. He says it has been around for years, starting with skiers and quickly spreading to snowboarders.

"It's a run from the top of the mountain to the lodge, 'beat you to the bottom,' " Frederick explains. "The rules are that there are no rules. You just have to get there first."

But boarder-cross *per se* was kind of discovered by accident. A Canadian filmmaker by the name of Greg Stump was up in Whistler, Canada, several years ago filming a snowboarding obstacle-course event. Suddenly, he had an idea. He grabbed five or six of the competitors and asked them to come down the obstacle course together while he was filming. Naturally, there was some pushing and shoving, and all the competitors finished with smiles on their faces. They enjoyed it. It was tough, competitive, and a whole lot of fun.

Pretty soon, boarder-cross courses were being set up in many places. They were constructed down the fall line of the mountain, but with banks, berms, *whoop-di-doos* (little rollers set up one after another), and single, double, and triple jumps along the way. Some of the course is set up top to bottom, other parts move sideways. So it's a real zigzag trip down the hill. There are also hay bales, double platform jumps, and gates to mark the course.

There are no real rules so it's not surprising that a boarder-cross race contains a lot of physical contact. Elbows are often thrown and there is a lot of pushing and pulling. However, there are some limitations to keep things from getting out of hand. You can't literally push a guy over or pull him down. And you can't grab and hold. But there is plenty of banging of bodies on the way down.

Boarder-cross has become a great spectator sport. Part of the appeal is its unpredictability. Unlike the giant slalom or halfpipe, where there are usually distinct favorites, you never know who's going to win a boarder-cross race. There may be four of the world's best snowboarders in the field and one amateur. But a situation can develop where the four elite riders are going head-to-head, tangling and bumping one another over the hills, and the amateur can sneak right past them to get the checkered flag.

The runs usually take between forty-five seconds and one minute to complete. If there are heats, the first two finishers in each heat will get into the finals. If it's just a single race, then, of course, there is just one winner. Alpine riders will use their racing boards when competing in boarder-cross, while the freestylers stick with their boards. It depends on the roots of the competitor. While the majority are freestylers, boarder-cross is something everyone can do as a welcome change of pace and a chance to have fun and let off some steam at the same time.

There are boundaries on the course, a path the competitors must follow. If someone goes out of bounds, he must re-enter the course at the point he left it, otherwise he is disqualified. There is usually a course marshall to oversee the race, and several officials up and down the course. Some of the courses wind around so much that there must be officials at blind spots. Riders must also wear a helmet when competing in this event.

Boarder-cross courses are actually constructed on a manicured, flat run. Banks and jumps are made by piling up snow, while racing gates are set fifteen or twenty feet apart to mark the turns. Once the course is set up, riders often flock to race on it, just for fun if nothing else. Plus it's another way for riders to renew rivalries.

"There has always been a rivalry between Alpine riders and freestylers," says Shawn Frederick, who has competed in boarder-cross as well as photographed it. "In addition, it's a chance for riders to go against those they usually compete against in the slalom or halfpipe. Now they are all boarder-crossers for that day and they can take out all their anxieties and frustrations on the course.

"It's also unique because suddenly there's the world champion Alpine rider and the world champion freestyler pushing and elbowing each other on the boarder-cross course. They're mixing it up together, suddenly equals where nothing matters except crossing the finish line first."

Both men and women compete in this unique snowboarding event. Occasionally, women and men have even run the course together. But the discipline is still not a sanctioned event, nor part of the national tour or World Cup. It's more like a specialty event and is run as such during some competitions. A few independent companies are beginning to put on their own contests now and boarder-cross is more likely to be seen in this kind of competition. There has been talk about sanctioning the discipline, but that may not happen for a while.

"I don't care for boarder-cross as a sanctioned event," says Rick Waring. "I just don't visualize corporate America supporting six guys hitting each other on the head or trying to push each other into a tree. It's too much like Roller Derby."

More likely, boarder-cross will remain a fun event, a way to release tensions and enjoy another facet of the sport. In some ways, it's almost like a bunch of guys deciding to play a choose-up game of basketball, three-on-three. It's not unusual for a group to go to the boarder-cross course and just let it all hang out, no officials, no crowd, just a lot of good fun.

When should a relative newcomer to the sport take a shot at boarder-cross? Not too quickly, according to Shawn Frederick:

"Take the competitiveness of boarder-cross away," Frederick says, "and you still have an obstacle course in front of you. If you can go down the mountain as fast as you can over bumps, banks, jumps, and turns, and if you feel up to the level of the course, then go for it. But if your ability isn't up to the course, then don't."

But in boarder-cross there is an equalizer. The discipline has been described as fifty percent ability, thirty percent balance, and twenty percent courage and physical toughness. So you don't have to be the world's best snowboarder to win it.

28 BOARDER-CROSS.

Boarder-cross may not be a sanctioned discipline, but more and more riders are trying it and enjoying it. It also doesn't hurt that more spectators are attending. So it's pretty safe to say that it is a part of snowboarding that is here to stay.

EXTREME SNOWBOARDING

Extreme snowboarding is in a class all by itself. It is so far removed from the other disciplines that it sometimes seems to be a separate sport. Venturing into the world of the extreme takes incredible skill, knowledge, courage, conditioning, confidence, and daring. It is not for the novice; it is not for the faint of heart; and it is definitely not something to be done on a dare or a bet. Extreme snowboarding is serious business. In some cases, it can be deadly serious.

Someone riding extreme must be an advanced expert snowboarder, a person who will be completely in command of any terrain he may encounter. However, the catch-22 is that he never knows what he may encounter. There is nothing predictable about extreme snowboarding.

To reach the starting point, an extremist may have to go in by helicopter. Or he may have to hike or backpack to his destination. Sometimes, an extremist will go to the top resort on a mountain. There may still be another two thousand or three thousand vertical feet to the summit of the mountain and that's where the extremist wants to go. So he'll hike up to the spine of the ridge. This, in itself, can be dangerous.

There are some additional prerequisites for the extreme snowboarder. He's got to know a lot more than just how to handle his board. He has to be well tuned to Mother Nature and has to understand the risks and safety factors involved in what he's doing. For one thing, he must have a thorough understanding of snow and what it does.

Snow falls vertically. But when it settles on a mountain it settles horizontally. Sometimes there is a snowfall that is so dry it remains vertical when it hits the surface. It just doesn't have the wet heaviness to settle in. Those kinds of conditions can easily result in an avalanche. An avalanche happens when a pile of dry, fluffy snow begins moving after something like a loud boom or shockwave unsettles it.

Sometimes there will be a wet, heavy snow on top of the dry, vertical fluffy snow. Again, it's easy for an avalanche to start, because the heavy snow can cause the light snow four or five feet underneath to collapse under it.

So the extreme snowboarder must have an exceptional knowledge of the mountain, of snow, and of snow texture. The snowfall can be different on every mountain and in every part of the world. The temperature and humidity can also be different. Some snow is wet, some dry, some flaky, and some like corn. The extremist must understand every facet of a snowfall. That knowledge could save him from injury or worse.

There are some hard-and-fast rules that all extreme snowboarders must follow. Again, it's a matter of vital importance because of the safety factor. No one, for instance, should ever venture into the extreme alone. Never ride extremes without an extreme guide. Be sure to go with someone who knows the terrain. The guide will always go first, no *ifs, ands,* or *buts.*

If the guide wants to try a new mountain, he will always take some of his buddies with him. They're the top men who know what they're doing, know how to handle emergencies and are always looking out for one another. No one goes off by himself.

The extremes are always out-of-bounds, often unchartered and unpatrolled areas. It's mandatory that anyone in these areas carry an avalanche transceiver. This is a small electronic device that is strapped to the rider's body. If he gets buried in an avalanche the transceiver will begin sending a signal so there is a chance he can be found.

Sometimes extreme riders will be dropped into a certain area by helicopter just to ride one section of the mountain. Then the helicopter will pick them up again. So extreme snowboarding can be a fifteen-minute run, or it can be a three-hour run.

Shawn Frederick has done some extreme snowboarding, though he doesn't consider himself close to expert. What he has done, however, is to photograph some of the top people in action and that has given him some firsthand impressions of this daring discipline.

"The key to extreme is the uncertainty of the snow combined with a near-vertical descent," Frederick says. "It's almost like free-falling. The only thing that's basically suspending you up in the air is that little metal edge that's digging into the snow. That, and your body positioning.

"I've been in situations when I've just put my weight a little too far forward and at the snap of a finger I was head over heels, head over heels, maybe forty or fifty times, to the bottom. Once you fall in that kind of situation you can't stop."

Frederick says the worst thing someone can do when they fall in the extreme is panic and tighten up. You've got to be more like a Raggedy Ann doll. There is less chance of being hurt that way.

"Many times when you go head over heels in the extreme you instantly create a mini-avalanche," Frederick says. "That can be dangerous. I would say that maybe half the time you fall in the extreme, you end up with four or five feet of snow on top of you. So if you go, just ride with it. Sometimes you can ride out of it."

Why do snowboarders want to take this ultimate challenge? It's hard to say. Maybe it's man's passion to challenge Mother Nature, to conquer the unconquerable. For many, it's the ultimate high, the ultimate rush. The extremist starts his run and doesn't know what to expect.

"The snow blends with the human eye when you ski or snowboard down a hill," says Shawn Frederick, "so you can't always see what's in front of you. In a ski resort, the signs are posted: Cliff. Rock. Stay Back. Out of Bounds. When you're in the extreme there are no signs, no first aid kits, no ski patrols, nothing there. That's the rush of the whole thing. It's a complete whiteout. You're on such a steep, steep run. The smart extremist, therefore, will check out the run before he starts down. He can either hike up the descent route or check it out by helicopter. To look at a run from twelve thousand feet below is one thing. When you look at it from the top, it's a completely different effect.

"I'll say one other thing: Snowboarding in the extremes takes an incredible amount of confidence. I don't even think it's courage. Just an incredible amount of confidence that far surpasses that of the average person."

When an extremist gets to his starting point, he generally is not going to ride down clear, open, snow-powder fields. He's more likely going to be on the vertical part of a mountain piled with snow and full of chutes and *couloirs. Couloir* is the French word for an extreme chute. This is real vertical stuff.

According to experts, a typical extreme run would have the rider drop in over a *cornice*. A cornice is found at the top of the mountain, created when the wind whips up the face of the mountain, creating a vertical rise of snow that soon freezes. On a small hill, a cornice might be just five feet high. But in some extreme places, the cornices are forty or fifty feet high, and sometimes beyond vertical.

After riding the cornice, the snowboarder might enter a narrow *couloir.* While he must keep from falling forward, he often has to also jump over and go around rocks. Again, it's almost like a free fall, with the edge of the board the only thing keeping the extremist upright and riding. He might then traverse a series of chutes and extreme vertical drop-offs.

There are also hills and sometimes even cliffs from which the rider will jump off. Some of the cliffs present still another danger. None of the top extreme riders will blindside a cliff. They have to know what's below. So these major jumps are completely inspected beforehand, with particular attention to the landing area.

"Compared to an extremist's jumps, ski jumping is wimpy," Shawn Frederick says. "Many of the extreme runs are inverted cliffs which, if you simply fell off, would kill you. Yet these guys are literally jumping off on their snowboards, landing, and continuing on their way."

The key factor, according to Frederick, is to have a very, very steep landing with a run-out. If a rider jumps a fifty-foot cliff, his body may be traveling forty or fifty miles per hour at the point of landing. So he's got to have that steep run-out to keep going. If he simply lands on a flat surface he will be seriously injured.

If the run-out leads right into a forest, the jumper may end up wrapped

29 GREG TOMLINSON PUSHES HIS TALENT OVER THE EDGE OF A MONTANA CLIFF,
ILLUSTRATING AN EXAMPLE OF EXTREME SNOWBOARDING.

around a tree; he's got to have one hundred yards to run out the jump. There also has to be a lot of snow—fresh powder, and very deep to cushion the blow. With deep snow and the proper run-out, the experts say it's possible to jump a three-hundred-foot cliff. At that point, it simply becomes a matter of courage.

Some of the top extreme riders today are Steve Matthews, Evan Feen, Damian Sanders, Craig Kelly, Steve Graham, and Dave Seone. Most of them have sponsors and are paid very well for going into the extremes. But then again, there are some guys who do it just for the fun, or the thrill of it.

"I heard that Damian Sanders once jumped from a cornice into a narrow couloir," says Shawn Frederick, "and while he was in the air, he suddenly did a backflip. Then he landed and continued on down. That's how very good these guys are. They're almost like naturalists. They respect the land and they understand it."

Frederick also says that some of the extreme guys grew up around these steep mountains and glaciers. They were the only source of recreation available to these guys and they quickly learned what the mountains were like and how to travel on them.

"I wouldn't recommend someone in Southern California who rides the mountains there to suddenly decide to go to Alaska or British Columbia, get in a helicopter, jump out on a mountaintop, and go," Frederick cautions.

One of the most renowned extreme areas is in Blue River, British Columbia, in Canada. There are three thousand square miles of mountain ranges there, called Mike Wigley's Helischeme. There are no chairlifts, no ski areas. The mountains are only accessible by helicopter. The helicopter will drop a rider off on one of the various ridges, let him run for ten or fifteen minutes, and then pick him up again.

Extreme snowboarding, however, is not for just a chosen few. Like the rest of the sport, it is growing and becoming more popular. In April of 1992, the very first extreme championship was held in the north glaciers of Valdez, Alaska. It wasn't an easy thing to judge. The winner, Mike "Tex" Davenport, of Mt. Baker, Washington, was the rider who took the most extreme line down the ridge. He was judged on his route down the ridge and his style.

So an extreme snowboarder has to be many things. He has to be wildly confident to begin with. On top of that, he has to be absolutely skilled on the board, ready to meet any emergency or extreme situation. He also might have to be a mountain climber, and a survivalist. He must cope with blizzards, avalanches, and any other extreme weather condition. He must know the mountain, the texture of the snow, and recognize danger before he is upon it.

If he qualifies in all these things, he can then go up and get the most incredible, ultimate high that his sport has to offer.

PART FIVE

1992 WOMEN'S UNITED STATES HALFPIPE CHAMPION SHANNON DUNN.

SNOWBOARDING CAMPS
AND THE PRO LIFE

SNOWBOARDING CAMPS

SPORTS camps have been part of the landscape for some time now. During the summer months, kids from all over the United States have a chance to pursue their favorite sport at a camp, usually going for one- or two-week sessions. The major sports—baseball, football, basketball—were featured in the early sports camps. And the campers usually had a chance to work with some of the biggest names from each sport.

Snowboarding has quickly taken a page out of the sports-camp book. During the last few years, a number of camps have sprung up during the off-season. Unfortunately, there is a decided lack of snow during the summer months in most areas of the United States, so there is a limit to just where the camps can be held.

A number of these snowboard camps are held on Mount Hood in Oregon. The reason is simple: There is ample snow there. On the southern face of Mount Hood sits the remnants of an old glacier, called the Palmer Glacier. Now it has been downgraded to the Palmer Snowfield, but there is still enough snow to make the area a popular summer training ground for winter sports. The national ski team, for instance, has trained on Mount Hood for years.

In 1988, the United States Snowboard Training Center (USSTC) began operating a snowboard camp on Mount Snow, Vermont. Since that time, a number of other camps have opened, but the USSTC operation remains unique for its intensity and objectives. Under the leadership of camp director Bob Gille, the camp not only provides an opportunity for campers to learn snowboarding, but offers other positive values as well.

"We run a very structured program," explains Bob Gille. "My own experience in the Marine Corps taught me that if you're sharing with people and you get much over five people you begin to lose base because of differences in personality. The more talkative person, the more assertive person, the more good-looking person gets the most attention. To counter that tendency, we limit our operation to a five-to-one ratio and this way we're able to get a real personal interaction between coaches and students."

Campers are grouped by ability, not by age or sex. Since the camp is open to everyone, there are both youngsters and adults attending each session. Gille says that the campers are predominately intermediate and advanced riders; perhaps twenty percent are beginners.

"By grouping the campers by ability, a twelve-year-old kid might be in the same group as a person of forty," said Gille. "What occurs here is that this enormous, interesting, self-support group generates. There is no generation gap because the people in the group are only relating to each other on the hill. You like snowboarding and he likes snowboarding, and that's all that matters."

Once the campers are in groups, the coaches go to work and attempt to implement the overall philosophy of the camp:

"Our goal," Bob Gille explained, "is to create an environment where people challenge their limits. And through challenging their limits, we hope they'll achieve interpersonal self-esteem. Using a structured environment and giving them some real basics of snowboarding, we urge them to challenge their limits and to feel good about who they are."

This might not sound like the average sports camp. Its objective is more ambitious because Bob Gille is trying to impart values through sport (in this case, snowboarding) that will carry over to other phases of the camper's life. He feels that many sports camps, including some other snowboarding facilities, are little more than recreational camps. The kids have a good time, but besides getting some coaching they do a lot of partying and look at it like a vacation away from home. He feels that his USSTC camp appeals to a small percentage who want to get serious and challenge their goals.

All the coaches are professionals and they aren't there simply to baby-sit or entertain the campers. They are there to teach, and both coach and camper work on the snow all day long.

Everyone wakes up at 6:30 A.M. Breakfast is served, restaurant style, until 7:15. At 7:30, everyone leaves to go up on the hill. They're on the snow by 8:00 A.M. All morning, the campers work on Alpine racing techniques and have intense slalom training. There is a break for lunch, and in the afternoon everyone moves to halfpipe training until 4:00 or 4:15 P.M. But the day isn't over yet.

There is a brief period to relax. The campers can play Ping-Pong, work on the trampoline or even skateboard. There are a number of skateboarding ramps on the site. Then, after dinner there is a video review of all the day's activities and the coaches talk to the campers. That takes about another hour and a half.

"By then everyone is pretty much tired," says Gille. "They have had a long, very hard day."

Many of Gille's coaches are top pros and champions during the professional touring season. But while they are world famous within snowboarding circles, they are simply coaches to the campers.

"Even though these are world-famous professional competitors, we don't stress the fact that they are big names," says Gille. "Some camps emphasize the superstar coach. The campers hang out with him and want to be with him. But I tell even the big stars that they aren't here to be a big star, but rather, a good coach. So while I've got top guys, they work for a lot less than they normally would because they're here to share an experience and spread the sport."

There is obviously a concentrated effort to make this a real snowboarding camp. The sport dominates the week. By the final Friday and Saturday, there are mini-competitions for the campers, giving them a chance to challenge themselves and to assess the progress they have made during the week. It's a competitive ending to a tiring but profitable week. And it's a great way to become a better snowboarder.

Running ten camps during the summer is not the only thing that Bob Gille and the USSTC do. Gille wants this still-young sport go in the right direction.

"I've often asked people involved with snowboarding if they want to have it as a professional sport or simply as theater. They have to decide at some point how they want it to go."

The USSTC also started a judging program about three years ago, trying to establish consistent and reasonable judging standards. Gille feels that snowboarding is fighting some of the same problems found with skateboarding or, for that matter, any sport that's still in its infancy.

"I've watched some young kids get their hearts broken by what I thought was poor judging," he says. "When you see kids being hurt like that it really gets to you and I felt I had to do something about it."

The USSTC is also fighting what Bob Gille perceives as a "bad-boy image," given to the sport by some magazines and media. It's like street-style skateboarding, where the prevailing perception is that the wrong kind of kids are involved with the sport, or that the sport is creating the wrong kind of kids.

"I respect that that's an element of the industry and an element of the sport," Gille says. "I just don't want it to be the dominant element. I want to increase an awareness of the element I represent."

But it is the summer camps that are really making an impact. Campers are getting both basic and advanced skills. They are also encouraged to push themselves and take risks. That, says Gille, will enable them to learn more.

"We really emphasize the basics," says Gille. "Some campers have said, 'But I already know how to do this.' Yet this is how we approach snowboarding. We want people to use all the basics to challenge themselves. Then they can try some new maneuvers and break some new ground.

"We challenge everybody to do it. Push themselves totally. But they can also have a cranking good time here. People leave feeling good about themselves. In fact, many of my campers return and many have said it's the greatest time they've had in their lives."

PROFESSIONAL SNOWBOARDING

Snowboarding as a professional sport is starting to come into its own. But in reality, the sport is just entering its second phase, coming out of its infancy. Prize money on the tours has not yet stabilized, and, in 1991, was actually down due to the overall economy. Some of the sponsors dropped out or cut back.

But, as Rick Waring said earlier, corporate America is becoming more intrigued by and interested in the sport. Television continues to showcase the Alpine and halfpipe events, and more competitors are looking to join the top group, the elite pros. Recreationally, snowboarding is growing by leaps and bounds. There is no reason to think the professional side of the sport won't continue to grow.

World-class Alpine skiers have been national heroes for years, even when they had to operate under the guise of being amateurs. In today's economy, skiers from the United States, Canada, Japan, Italy, France, Germany, Austria, and other countries command huge fees in endorsements and winning contests. There's no reason to think snowboarders won't soon join them.

Of course, in the early days of the sport, it was a very different story. The pros back then were like pioneers who knew they wouldn't make much money. Nor did they have the comforts of home via fancy ski lodges. On the contrary, they often traveled around in battered vans, sleeping in them, and scratching for every dollar as they drove to the few contests that were held in those days.

Don Szabo remembers some of what is considered the "old days" of the sport.

"It has only been the last three or four years that we have had a whole series of competitions like this," Szabo says. "There were always small competitions around, but I can remember many times when I started snowboarding that I was one of the only guys [on a snowboard] on the mountain.

"But even at competitions back then, we all had a good time. It didn't really matter who won. Everybody knew each other and we were all in the same boat. Prize money was just a few hundred dollars, so none of us was getting rich. I used to just drive around to the different competitions, from Tahoe to Colorado. It's gotten to the point now where it's very serious, but it was a real good time back then and I was glad to be a part of it."

Then, as now, most of the early pros were very young. They could endure the hardships. As Don Szabo says, "Life wasn't as serious then. Most of us were young and the few older guys really had some status. We all looked up to them."

Back then, Don Szabo and the other early pros didn't even think of the future of their sport. "I was just having a good time," he says.

But, as snowboarding began to grow up and become more organized, the early professionals had to grow up, too. Don Szabo, like the others, realized he would have to decide whether to stay in the sport or not.

"Eventually you figure you've got to do something," Szabo says. "It beats working nine-to-five, but it is a job. Fun, but still a job. Some people don't realize this. They look at me and the others and see how lucky we are to do this, that we're having fun all the time. But there's work involved."

Work and pressure. As a sport grows, it's the top people who make the most money, get the best sponsors and the most endorsements. So the pros have to stay in peak condition and always try to get better and better at what they do. For many of them, snowboarding has become a full-time job.

"This past season I did about eight or ten competitions," Don Szabo says. "During the off-season, I'm a coach at the United States Snowboarding Training Center where I work with Bob Gille. In between, we do photo shoots, promotions, and demonstrations. I represent a clothing and a board company, and also companies that make boots and sunglasses. The prize money was down this past year, so we've got to keep busy with other things."

Shannon Dunn is much newer to the professional scene, but she has heard the stories of the so-called old days, when the pros lived in their vans or even in tents.

"Those stories are all true," she says. "It was mostly men back then. There were a few women starting out, but not too many. And we're only talking about seven years ago or so."

Like many of the others, Dunn competed in ten or eleven events in the 1991–92 season, when the prize money was down. But she had a board and clothing company sponsoring her, and they helped to shoulder some of the burden. "They take care of my expenses," she says.

Like many of today's pros, Shannon Dunn is involved with snowboarding

30 1992 UNITED STATES ALPINE CHAMPION SHANNON MELHUSE.

for most of the year. During the summer she coaches at a snowboard camp and gives trampoline demonstrations on the East Coast. Yet she also finds time to attend the University of Colorado, something she hopes to continue.

"This is something a lot of the girls are doing," she says. "They go to school in the fall and finish up just in time to compete on the circuit."

Just nineteen when she began competing, Dunn was one of the younger pros on the circuit. She says the average age is from about twenty to twenty-two. "There's one girl competing at fifteen, but I don't think any of the girls is over thirty. I know there are still a few men competing at thirty-one or thirty-two and a lot who are twenty-six or twenty-seven."

The fraternity of professional snowboarders is still not a large one, especially when compared to other sports. And there still isn't enough money to go around to give the pros the kind of income that is made by those competing in sports like baseball, basketball, tennis, and golf, among others. But those committed to the sport stay with it all year round.

"There used to be a big off-season," says Rick Waring, "but now most people are running snowboard camps and doing other things like representing their sponsors with demos and photo shoots. I would say that probably the top thirty performers in each discipline make a pretty good living. A lot of them have signature models [boards] and are beginning to see a residual effect from their names.

"But it's a full-time job. They hit trade shows during the off-season and many are now doing videos. And the more popular the sport becomes, the longer the season will be because there will be competitions in more parts of the world.

"Right now, I would say the thirtieth guy in all disciplines makes about $30,000 a year and the number one guy a little over $100,000 a year. The money for the women is very comparable."

The future of professional snowboarding hinges on a number of things: Will the sport get into the Olympics? Will more corporate sponsors jump on the bandwagon and take the prize money to a new level? Will television increase its coverage of the sport? Will the ski companies continue to become involved with snowboarding? All of the above will not only serve to help today's professionals, but will also lead to creating the pros of tomorrow.

Exposure is the key to any new sport. Introducing it to youngsters at an early age is the best way to insure the future. To share the feelings of the top pros—the rush of excitement they get from carving down the mountain, competing in the halfpipe, sliding over logs and racing through gates—is to encourage others to try it.

And to try snowboarding is to love it. That seems to be a universal credo as far as this sport is concerned. You don't have to be a professional to enjoy it. You don't have to do handplants in the halfpipe or charge down a boarder-cross course or Ollie over a fallen tree. You can simply carve your way down a mountain, looking relaxed and majestic, and leave a beautiful trail of powdery white snow as a sign that you were there.

Maybe that's all you'll ever want to do. But the rest of it is there too, for those who want it.

For the sport of snowboarding, tomorrow is smiling brightly and it's beginning to look as if the future is now.

ABOUT THE AUTHOR

BILL GUTMAN has been a freelance writer since 1972. In that time, he has written more than 100 books, many of them in the sports field. His work includes profiles and biographies of sports stars, including recent works on Bo Jackson, Michael Jordan, David Robinson, and Magic Johnson. In addition, Mr. Gutman has written biographies of such non-sports personalities as former president Andrew Jackson and jazz immortal Duke Ellington.

He has also written seven novels for youngsters—many of which have sports themes—as well as specialized high-interest, low-vocabulary books. His adult books include the Magic Johnson biography, *Magic, More Than a Legend*; an autobiography with former New York Giants baseball star Bobby Thomson, and a re-creation of the 1951 Giants-Dodgers pennant race called *The Giants Win the Pennant! The Giants Win the Pennant!*; a collection of profiles of former major league baseball stars called *When the Cheering Stops,* as well as several basketball and baseball histories.

Prior to *Snowboarding,* Mr. Gutman has written instructional "how-to" books on twelve different sports in a series entitled *Go For It!* He currently lives in Poughquag, New York, with his wife, Cathy, two stepchildren, and a variety of pets.

ABOUT THE PHOTOGRAPHER

SHAWN FREDERICK, an action sports/commercial photographer, has captured some of the finest images in over twenty publications worldwide.

Shawn has photographed an enormous variety of landscapes and subjects—everything from the motion picture movie sets of Southern California to the white sands of South America. His work has been seen on covers and in editorial features in *Surfing, Swimwear Illustrated, Skateboarding, Snowboarder, National Geographic World,* and numerous fashion/glamour magazines. His clients include Rolex, Nissan, Ocean Pacific swimwear, Oakley Sunglasses, Bauer, Maska CCM, Mistral, and Miller Genuine Draft, accounts that have been the directing forces behind his photography-associated company since 1989.

Over the last three years, Shawn has traveled the globe in search of the best snowboarding terrain to photograph for *TransWorld Snowboarding* and *Snowboarder* magazines.

Shawn Frederick currently lives in Southern California and is an avid outdoor sportsman. Surfing is his favorite hobby.